李佩玲Bella ◎著

倍斯特出版事業有限公司 Ltd.

U0066503

愛玩客旅遊英語

無壓力學習法，輕鬆瘋玩旅遊景點
Fantastic and Enjoyable

三大旅遊「FUN」程式 ➡ 即學即用＋脫口而出 ➡ 旅遊英語不NG

● 瞭解地理人文知識：
精選28大旅遊景點，列出最詳盡的人文風景資訊

● 向英文母語人士偷師：
聽聽英文母語人士都怎麼聊，邊聽、邊學、邊玩效果加倍

● 學會與眾不同的回答：
特別設計(白目愛玩咖Michelle、帥氣冒險王Matt和精明小資女Becca)的三問三答，拓展應答思路，從容開口說英文

MP3

　　「為什麼你想要學英文呢？」我常常這麼問我的學生和朋友。大多數的人回答我，想要讓自己在職場上更有競爭力。但是近幾年來，越來越多的人告訴我：「我想要自助旅行。」或是：「人生苦短，我想要去看看這個世界。」我對於這些回答相當的有共鳴。學習英文本來就是以可以學以致用為主。托福、多益考得再高分，出國旅行時面對外國人還是只能恬恬玩猜猜樂，或是零零落落的和路人問答，真的令人很想翻桌。懂再多的單字和再高級的文法，對於旅遊主題不熟悉或是不精通旅遊行話，還是夢一場。

　　針對了這個需求，我們設計了這本以口說為主，旅遊為主題的「愛玩客旅遊英語」。

　　28 個旅遊主題搭配三個不同性格的人物，教你怎麼回答各式各樣的主題。針對每一個主題我們提供了背景簡介，生動對話，旅遊主題問答以及道地旅遊片語重點提示，讓你出門只要帶背包和嘴巴就好囉！GO！

Bella Lee

　　愛玩客的旅遊英語的架構上包含了背景起源、情境對話和三問三答，期許讀者以最無壓力的方式學習旅遊英語。

　　教科書對話和實際口說運用上的落差，相信許多英語學習者都曾經歷過。在與當地人交談時，更不時碰到有口難言的情況，也並未展現出自己實際的口語水平。在口試時更無法輕鬆的談談自己旅遊的經驗。而此書的三問三答設計了三個人物。提供了讀者在同一話題中三個實際問題與三個不同的思考的方向。由不同角度切入話題，大幅拓展英語應答思路！！！

『三問三答的三個主角』

◎白目愛玩咖 Michelle：無厘頭、妙語連珠、犀利、又帶點詼諧且不切實際的方式。

◎帥氣冒險王 Matt：中肯、實際、魅力十足的背包客口吻。

◎精明小資女 Becca：富創意、趣味性十足、具個人特色的表達。

編輯部　敬上

Contents
目次

Unit ① Waterfall
瀑布

背景起源

It always makes people's face light up when they come upon a waterfall at the end of the hike. It is like a special treat of nature, the icing on the cake of a good walk in the woods. It doesn't matter if it is a trickle or a torrent. People are drawn to either one for different reasons. Maybe it's the variety that's the real lure. And a single waterfall can be very different throughout the year and from year to year. On a hot summer day, they're a blast to play in. Nothing seems better when the running fresh, chilly water pour upon you from the waterfall on a hot day. Creek walking also allows you to get intimate with the waterfalls. What's your favorite part about waterfalls?

　　每當大家在健行的終點看見瀑布時，眼睛都會瞬間發亮。那就像是大自然給我們的特別的禮物，或是蛋糕上面的糖霜一樣好上加好的美好。不論是一個細流或是狂奔的流水，大家都還是因為不一樣的原因而被瀑布吸引著。或許變化才是真正的誘餌。而一個瀑布在一年之間會有很多變化，每年也都會變得不一樣。在一個炎熱的夏日，在瀑布裡也可以玩得十分開心。好像沒有什麼是比在很熱的一天，被清新、冰涼的瀑布水沖倒到你的頭上還要美好。在小溪間行走也可以讓你和瀑布變得更親密。那你最喜歡瀑布的原因又是什麼呢？

Dialogue 情境對話 　MP3 01

Ian and Derrick are hiking at the Watkins Glen State Park, New York.
伊恩和德瑞克正在紐約的沃特金斯峽谷州立公園健行。

Ian: This place is gorgeous.

伊恩：這個地方真美。

Derrick: Yeah, this is one of the best spots around this area. I love coming out here and take my mind off things.

德瑞克：對啊，這是這地區最好的景點之一。我很喜歡來這裡靜一靜。

Ian: Except that you can't really do that because it's so crowded here.

伊恩：但是你不能真的靜一靜因為這裡也太多人了吧！

Derrick: haha...no, I can't do that now. It is really crowded today.

德瑞克：哈哈…現在真的不行。今天真的很多

人耶。

Ian: It's like an international fair or something. You can see people from everywhere here.

伊恩：這裡好像是國際園遊會還是什麼的。在這裡可以看到來自各處的人。

Derrick: Yeah, this place is a big tourist attraction.

德瑞克：對啊，這地方是一個很大的觀光景點。

Ian: It's not hard for me to see why. This place is just beautiful. We are passing under the waterfalls and going around then. How many waterfalls are there anywhere?

伊恩：嗯一看就知道了。這地方那麼漂亮。我們從瀑布下走過，或是繞過瀑布。這裡到底有多少個瀑布啊？

Derrick: I think 19! I just looked it up the other day.

德瑞克：我想是十九個！我前幾天才查過。

Ian: And this gorge is just beautiful to look at. I wish the camera could capture its beauty, but it's just so grand for the camera to capture it all.

伊恩：而且這峽谷看起來真的很美。我真希望相機可以捕捉它的美，但是這裡真的是太大了。相機拍不起來。

Derrick: There are a lot of professional photographers that like to come out here and take pictures. Just google them.

德瑞克：這裡有很多專業攝影師喜歡來拍照。Google 就好啦。

Ian: That's not what I meant, Derrick. I mean...it's just not gonna be the same as this right in front of us. You know what I mean?

伊恩：我不是那個意思啦德瑞克。我的意思是說…相片跟現在在我們眼前的這個美景是不會一樣的啦。

Derrick: I guess you're right. We just have to take mental pictures.

德瑞克：嗯我想你是對的。我們只好在心裡記起來囉。

Ian: Yeah, I guess so! Get ready to get wet again, here comes another waterfall!

伊恩：對啊，我想也是！欸準備好被潑溼了噢！又有另外一個瀑布了！

01
Question

What's your favorite waterfall? Why?
你最喜歡的瀑布是哪一個？為什麼呢？

Michelle
蜜雪兒

Niagara Falls is my favorite waterfalls. The falls are big, beautiful and very loud. And you get to travel to New York and Canada since it's right in the middle of the two places. At nighttime the falls are even lighted up with colorful lights. I'm definitely going there for my honeymoon. It's just very romantic in general.

尼加拉瓜瀑布是我最喜歡的瀑布。那裡的瀑布又大，又美，而且超大聲的。而且你還可以順便去紐約或是加拿大旅行，因為它剛好在兩個地方的中間。在晚上的時候他們還會有不一樣顏色的燈亮起。我一定要去那裡度蜜月。整體來說那就是一個很浪漫的地方啊。

Matt
麥特

My favorite one is Victoria Falls in Africa. It's one of the Seven Natural Wonders of the world, and it's so easy to see why once you're there. The hardest part is to get there I guess. It is one of the largest and most inspiring in the world. The waterfall is about 108 meters long. I am still in awe of it.

　我最喜歡的是在非洲的維多利亞瀑布。那是世界七大奇景之一，而且一旦你到了那裡之後你就會很輕易地知道為什麼它是七大奇景之一。我想最難的地方就是要先到非洲吧。那是世界上最大也是最激勵人心的瀑布之一。整個瀑布大概有一百八十公尺長。我到現在還是覺得很驚人。

Becca
貝卡

I really like the Rainbow Falls at Big Island, Hawaii. Just like its name suggests, the rainbow can be seen every sunny morning at around 10 am. The waterfall flows over a natural lava cave, which was believed to be one of the

Hawaiian goddess's home. How romantic is that?

　　我真的很喜歡在夏威夷大島的彩虹瀑布。就像它的名字一樣，每個晴天的早上十點左右都可以看到彩虹。瀑布是從天然的火山岩洞穴傾流而下，那個洞穴也聽說是夏威夷一個女神的家。真的超浪漫的！

02
Question

What do you usually like to do at the waterfalls?
你通常都喜歡在瀑布做什麼呢？

Michelle
蜜雪兒

　　I usually try to find the best angle to take a picture with the waterfall. That's all it's about for me really. I finally make it that far to the waterfall, and all I really want is to have a decent picture with the waterfall. It's a good incentive to hike to the waterfall for me.

　　我通常都會試著找跟瀑布照相最好的角度。對我來說那是最重要的。我好不容易才到了瀑布，而且我真正最想要的只是一張跟瀑布的漂亮合照。對我來說那是健行到瀑布很好的動力。

Matt
麥特

There are so many things you can do at the waterfall. My friends and I like to jump off the rock and swim. When the water is clean, it is the most refreshing feeling you get. We usually do <u>cannon ball</u> or just dive under the waterfall. Of Course, we only jump off when it is safe at that place.

在瀑布有很多事情可以做啊。我的朋友跟我都很喜歡從石頭上跳下去游泳。當水很乾淨的時候,那是最令人覺得清新的感覺。我們通常都會抱膝跳水製造很大的水花或是潛到瀑布底下。當然那是在安全的狀況之下我們才會跳水啦。

Becca
貝卡

I usually hike to the waterfall, and swim around when it's safe. Or I would <u>take a step back</u> and just try to take everything in. Sometimes I like to meditate on the rock while listening to the waterfall. It's like one of those nature sounds CDs only it's real there.

我通常會健行到瀑布，然後安全的話還會到處游游。或者我會退一步，然後就把那美景盡收眼底。有的時候我也喜歡聽著瀑布的聲音然後坐在岩石上面打坐。那就好像是在聽那些大自然的聲音 CD 一樣。

03
Question

What do you love or hate about waterfalls?
你喜歡或是不喜歡瀑布的哪裡呢？

Michelle
蜜雪兒

I love how beautiful the waterfalls are naturally, but I really hate how dangerous the hike can be sometimes. The hike is usually wet and muddy. A lot of slipping and sliding skills are required. Often a lot of accidents happen each year. I don't understand why no more security measures are in play.

我當然很喜歡瀑布有多麼的漂亮，但是有的時候我也真的很討厭去瀑布的步道有多危險。那個步道通常都是很濕又很多泥巴。會需要用到滑來滑去的技能。而且每年也都有很多意外會發生。我真的不懂為什麼沒有更多的安全措施。

Matt
麥特

It's just amazing to see what nature can offer. The huge body of water happens to fall with the perfectly vertical rock, creating one of the most beautiful sceneries in the world. Who would have thought that we are so easy to entertain? God must be a pretty smart parent...

就真的很神奇可以看到大自然製造出來的東西。這麼多的水剛好隨著那垂直的石頭落下，創造出來世界上最漂亮的美景之一。誰想得到我們會那麼好娛樂？神一定是一個很聰明的父母親…

Becca
貝卡

Besides the fact that it's usually free, waterfalls are actually very beneficial for our bodies. The moving water results in negative ions. Somehow these negative ions result in increased serotonin levels in our brain, which makes us more relaxed and happier. Natural remedy for a stressed office lady right there!

　　除了它通常都是免費的之外，瀑布也有很多對我們身體很有益處的地方。流動的水製造了負離子，然後這些負離子就使得我們頭腦裡的血清激素增高，因為那樣我們就會覺得更加放鬆，或是更開心。那就是大自然對壓力很大的上班族的天然療癒啊！

 Useful expressions

⛵ **one's face lights up** 讓某人的眼睛為之一亮；讓某人開心的

❶ Her face lights up just by the sight of him.
一看到他，她的眼睛為之一亮。

⛵ **drawn to** 被⋯吸引

❷ He is always drawn to troubles.
他總是跟麻煩扯上關係。

⛵ **Seven Natural Wonders** 世界七大奇景

❸ The Seven Natural Wonders are all on my bucket list.
世界七大奇景都在我死前要做的事情的清單裡面。

⛵ **in awe of** 對⋯感到震驚，敬畏的

❹ He is always in awe of her.
他總是對她感到很敬畏。

⛵ **cannon ball** 抱膝跳水

❺ Let's do a cannon ball off the boat!!

我們來從船上抱膝跳水吧！！

⛵ **take a step back** 退後一步

❻ You need to take a step back and think about the whole thing.

你應該要退後一步，想想看整件事。

⛵ **result in** 造成

❼ His procrastination results in a lot more work for other workers in the office.

他的拖延造成辦公室裡其他人的工作大增。

⛵ **natural remedy** 天然療法

❽ Lemon juice and ginger is a common cold natural remedy.

檸檬汁和薑是一種感冒常見的天然療法。

2 Lake
湖

Unit

 背景起源

A lake is surrounded by lands, and usually separated from the ocean and other rivers. While most people daydream about beaches, some claim that beaches are overrated. You don't get all sandy and there is really no need to rinse off when you just jump in the fresh water. (When it's clean of course). There are all sorts of activities you can do on a lake, such as standing up paddling, fishing, tubing, wakeboarding, jet skiing, or taking a nap by the lake on a sleepy afternoon. You just have to be creative, and you will find out there is so much a lake can offer; even the mystery of Nessie, also known as the Loch Ness Monster. A lake also symbolizes calmness. Perhaps it's the glassy, mirror-like water, or the scenery you see in the reflection of the lake, the intangible tranquility you feel just in the presence of a lake is incredibly soothing.

　　湖泊是被陸地包圍，而且通常和海洋還有其他的河流分開。當很多人正想著海邊作白日夢的時候，也有很多人說海邊其實沒那麼好。如果你跳入淡水（當然是當它很乾淨的時候）你不會弄得全身都是沙子，而且上岸也真的不用再沖洗過。在湖上你可以做各式各樣的活動，例如 SUP（站立式划槳）、釣魚、玩拖曳圈、滑水和騎水上摩托車，或是在慵懶的午後在湖邊睡個午覺。只要你夠有創意，在湖邊真的有很多可以玩的；甚至還有流傳出 Nessie，或是大家所知道的尼斯湖水怪的傳說。湖也同時象徵著平靜。可能是因為像玻璃和鏡面般的湖水，或是湖水倒影裡的美麗風景，只要在湖泊面前就會感受到無形的寧靜，那是非常療癒的。

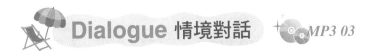

Dialogue 情境對話　　MP3 03

Sammy and Tyler are visiting Tyler's family at Keuka Lake, NY in the summer.
珊米和泰勒今年夏天正在拜訪泰勒在紐約，丘卡湖邊的家人。

Sammy: I can't believe you grew up at such a charming place. When you told me we were going to New York, all I could think of was the hustling bustling New York City.

珊米：我不敢相信你竟然是在這麼迷人的地方長大的。你跟我說我們要去紐約的時候，我只有想到忙碌的紐約市。

Tyler: <u>Tell me about it.</u> That's what everyone thinks of. Keuka Lake is

泰勒：我知道！大家都那麼想。丘卡湖是這邊

one of the Finger Lakes here. Frankly, I think it's the best one. Hehe. We used to go fishing every day when we were little. I started fishing when I was five.

Sammy: Really? That's incredible. That explains why you <u>are so into</u> fishing now. I see where that is coming from now.

Tyler: Yeah, not just that. There are so many things you can do here.

Sammy: What else can we do here?

Tyler: We can try wakeboarding if you're feeling adventurous. Or on a beautiful afternoon like this, my parents would take out the pontoon boat, and we would just cruise around the lake doing house window-shopping.

的指狀湖之一。老實說，我覺得是最棒的一個。嘿嘿⋯我們以前小的時候每天都會去釣魚。我從五歲就開始釣魚了。

珊米：真的假的？真是太棒了。難怪你現在那麼喜歡釣魚。我現在知道原因了。

泰勒：對啊，不只有釣魚，在這裡你可以做很多事。

珊米：在這裡我們還可以幹嘛？

泰勒：如果你想冒點險的話我們可以試試看滑水。或是在像這樣美好的午後，我爸媽會一邊開著駁船漫游著湖邊，一邊瀏覽在湖邊上的房子。

Sammy: Haha, that sounds like fun!

珊米：哈哈，聽起來很好玩！

Tyler: Of course, if you are in the mood of some wine, there are plenty of fantastic wineries here as well. Apparently the climate here is perfect for growing grapes.

泰勒：當然如果你想喝點小酒的話，這裡也有很多很棒的酒莊。很顯然這裡的氣候很適合種葡萄。

Sammy: Why not? We are on vacation. A little vino sounds great. Let me just take a shower and fresh up a little. We were on the flight for a long time. I stink.

珊米：有何不可。反正我們在渡假。一點小酒聽起來很不錯。先讓我洗個澡梳洗一下。我們在飛機上超久的。我好臭喔。

Tyler: Just take a lake shower! Come on! I'll jump in with you!

泰勒：跳到湖裡洗個澡就好啦！來啦！我陪你跳進去！

Sammy: Wait...What?!

珊米：等一下…你說什麼？！

湖

  *MP3 04*

Question

What are your impressions of a lake?
你對湖的印象是什麼？

 Michelle
蜜雪兒

Beautiful but boring. My cousin's family has a property by the lake in New Zealand. We visit them from time to time, but I just don't know what to do rather than sitting by the lake and get tanned. At first, I was impressed with the beautiful scenery, but then I thought to myself: "I would spend my money on somewhere else." I feel like I automatically get old when I'm by the lake. You know what I mean?

很美但是很無聊。我表姐他們家在紐西蘭的湖邊有棟房子。我們有時候會拜訪他們，可是我真的不知道除了坐在湖邊曬太陽之外還可以做什麼。一開始的時候我對那裡的美景很驚艷，可是後來我跟自己說：「我會把錢花在別的地方」。每次我在湖邊的時候我就覺得我好像自動老了好幾歲。你懂嗎？

Matt
麥特

湖

Campfire, fishing, and refreshing morning swims. I think it would be so awesome to just stay a few days or weeks by the lake. I was in the Boy Scout growing up, and we would spend our summer by the lake and learn how to fish and camp. The memory by the lake is definitely one of my favorite childhood memories. The buddy I met there is still one of my best friends.

營火、釣魚，還有清涼的晨泳。我覺得如果可以在湖邊待上個幾天或是幾個禮拜一定會超棒的。我小時候有加入童子軍，暑假的時候我們會在湖邊學怎麼釣魚還有露營。我最喜歡的兒時回憶之一就是暑假在湖邊的時光。我在那邊認識的一個朋友現在還是我最好的朋友之一。

Becca
貝卡

The lakes always give me an impression of calmness. I try to think about lakes when I'm really angry sometimes. It sounds funny but it really works. When I'm very stressed

about work, I'll try to think about lakes and it always brings me peace. I actually put a poster of a lake with the caption of "Keep Calm and Carry On" in front of my office desk.

湖總是給我一個很平靜的印象。有時候我很生氣的時候我就會試著想著湖。聽起來很好笑可是真的很有用。我如果工作壓力很大的時候我就會想像著湖泊，然後我就會平靜一些。其實我有在我辦公桌前貼了一張湖泊的海報，上面寫著：「保持冷靜，繼續前進。」

02 Question

Which lake do you want to visit? Why?
你最想要去哪一個湖？為什麼？

Michelle
蜜雪兒

Lake Louise! I saw it on the magazine randomly and I was very impressed with the hotel there. I heard it <u>costs a fortune to</u> stay there for a night, but I guess it's worth the money. I tried to call the travel agency about one of their tour packages there, but it's all booked out. I've already made a reservation for the next summer though. It's one of the most fancy hotels, so I have to <u>see it myself</u>.

露易絲湖！我有一次不小心在雜誌上看到就對那裡的飯店印象深刻。聽說在那住一晚超級貴，但我想應該是值得的。我有試著打給旅行社問他們那裡其中一個行程，可是全部都訂光了。但我有立刻下訂明年暑假去那裡的行程。那飯店是最豪華的飯店之一，我一定要親自瞧瞧。

湖

Matt
麥特

I've always wanted to go to the Loch Ness in Scotland. You know how it is! All those myths and legends you heard growing up. They just always fascinate me. When I first knew about Nessie, unlike everybody else, I was not surprised at all. I've always believed that there are some kinds of monsters in the lakes.

我一直都很想要去在蘇格蘭的尼斯湖。你懂得！從小聽說了那麼多關於它的神話和傳說。我總是對它很好奇。當我第一次聽到 Nessie 的時候，我沒有像其他人那麼驚訝。我一直都覺得在湖裡一定住著某種怪物。

Becca
貝卡

I heard about the Jellyfish Lake in Palau, and it really got me curious. It's pretty much a lake full of jellyfish. Sounds scary, but miraculously all the jellyfish isn't poisonous at all. Long story short, the jellyfish was originally from the ocean but the land rose, so the jellyfish was trapped in the lake. Overtime, they lost their predators, so there was no reason for them to be poisonous anymore. People can jump in the lake and swim with them without getting harmed. Palau is relatively cheaper to travel and their official language is English. Perfect.

我聽說過在帛琉的水母湖然後就一直對它很好奇。它其實就是一個充滿了水母的湖。聽起來很恐怖，可神奇的是在那裡所有的水母都沒有毒。長話短說就是本來那些水母來自海洋，直到有天陸地上升，所以那些水母就被困在湖泊裡。隨著時間過去，水母們失去了牠們的天敵，而也就沒有需要毒素的必要。人可以跳到湖裡跟牠們游泳也不會受傷。帛琉相對之下也是一個旅行比較便宜的地方，而且他們的官方語言是英文，太完美了。

Do you prefer to swim in the lake or in the ocean?

你比較想要在湖裡還是海裡游泳？

Michelle
蜜雪兒

Oh, I don't swim. I mean, I can swim, but I don't really swim. If swimming were only for the exercise purpose, why would I swim in the lake or ocean while there are swimming pools and gyms? Who knows what's in the ocean and lakes.

喔，我不游泳。我的意思是說，我會游泳，但我平常不會游泳。如果游泳只是為了運動，有健身房，我幹嘛要去湖裡或是海裡游泳？誰知道在海裡還有湖裡有什麼。

Matt
麥特

As much as I love the lakes, I prefer to swim in the ocean. There is something about the combination of the

sun and ocean. It always makes me so happy after I jump in the salty water. It's an instant stress relief for me.

　　儘管我很喜歡湖，我還是比較喜歡在海裡游泳。海和陽光有種令人無法解釋的元素。每次我跳入鹹鹹的海水之後總是很開心。對我來說那是一個即時減壓的辦法。

Becca
貝卡

I prefer swimming in the lake. It's just calm water, so I don't really have to worry about either the currents or the waves. It allows total relaxation. Better yet, you don't feel all sticky after swimming in the lake!

　　我比較喜歡在湖裡游泳。因為湖水很平靜，所以我不用擔心急流或是海浪。在湖裡游泳我才能真正的放鬆。更棒的是，在湖裡游泳以後也不會全身黏黏的。

Useful **expressions**

⚠ **in the presence of** 在…面前

❶ He always gets super sweaty and nervous talking in the presence of others.

他每次在別人面前說話的時候就會流很多汗和變得超級緊張。

⚠ **tell me about it** 我懂，我知道！

❷ Tell me about it! He never does his work well.

我知道！他從不做好他自己的工作。

⚠ **be into** 很喜歡…

❸ These people are super into running. I see them running everywhere.

這些人超喜歡跑步的。我到處都看得到他們在跑步。

⚠ **cost a fortune** …非常貴，花了很多錢

❹ It cost a fortune for him to fly to the other side of the world to see her.

他花了很多錢飛到世界的另一端去找她。

⚠ **see it myself** 親眼看到

❺ I don't believe what you said. I have to see it myself.

我不相信你說的話。我一定要親眼看到。

3 Cave 洞穴

Unit

Caves have been explored throughout the history. In the prehistory time, they were used for shelter, burial, or religious sites. Today researchers study caves because they can reveal stories and details of the past lives. Cavers explore them for the enjoyment of the activity or for physical exercise, such as rock climbing. For people who are less adventurous, a lot of the most beautiful underground caves have been changed into display caves, where lighting, floors, and other aids are installed to allow the tourists to experience the caves. Caves are way more than just holes in the ground. Some of them are quite fantastic. Discover your caveman spirits by visiting the caves!

　　一直以來洞穴就一直被人們探索著。在史前時代，洞穴是被用來當作是庇護所、掩埋場，或是宗教場地。現在研究學者們研究洞穴是因為洞穴可以透漏出以前生活的故事或是小細節。洞穴探索者喜歡洞穴是因為他們喜歡關於洞穴的運動，例如攀岩等等。對於沒有那麼熱愛冒險的人，也有很多地底下的美麗的洞穴被改為展示用的洞穴。在裡面會安裝燈光、地板，還有其他的輔助來幫助遊客體驗洞穴。洞穴並不是只是地底下的一個洞，它們有些是真的很棒的！去一些洞穴尋找你的野人精神吧！

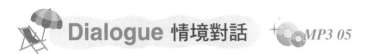

Dialogue 情境對話 ◦ MP3 05

Bell and her local friend Annie are visiting the Zipaquirá Salt Cathedral in Colombia.
貝兒和她當地的朋友安妮正在哥倫比亞的錫帕基拉鹽礦大教堂裡參觀。

Bell: This cave is a salt mine?	貝兒：這個洞穴是鹽礦嗎？
Annie: Yep, to be exact, it's a cathedral. We will see some sculptures that are made of salt soon.	安妮：對啊，說仔細一點這是一個大教堂。我們很快就會看到一些用鹽做成的雕像。
Bell: Wow, this is so impressive! Look at this, this is all salt on the wall. I was so wrong. I thought this was just another huge cave.	貝兒：哇，真是太厲害了！你看這個，在牆上這些都是鹽耶。我真是誤會大了。我以為這只是另一個普通的洞穴。

洞穴

Annie: Nope, it's a salt cathedral. It's actually really <u>mind blowing</u> to think that people did all this, I meant, dig out the salt, built the sculptures so that people can come and visit or pray.

安妮：不是喔，這是一個鹽礦大教堂。其實真的還蠻驚人的因為人們建造這一切，我是說，挖出鹽，建造雕像所以大家都可以來這裡參觀或是祈禱。

Bell: Oh it's dripping! Watch on for this part. It's pretty wet here.

貝兒：喔，在滴水！小心這個部分喔。這裡蠻濕的。

Annie: Thanks for the <u>heads up</u>! I have my hoodie on.

安妮：謝謝你的提醒啊！我有戴帽子啦！

Bell: This cave is gigantic. I feel like if I was not here with you, I would definitely get lost.

貝兒：這個洞穴也太大了吧。我覺得如果我不是因為跟你在一起的話，我一定會迷路的。

Annie: Stop being a <u>drama queen</u>. There are so many tourists. All you have to do is just ask them for directions. You will be fine. Go explore a little if you want. There is a lot to see here.

貝兒：不要那麼誇張啦。這裡有那麼多觀光客。你只要跟他們問方向就好啦！你會沒事的。如果你想要的話，去到處看看啊！這裡有很多可以參觀的。

Bell: I might go check out the altar at the back and pray a little.

貝兒：我想要去聖壇那裡看看，順便祈禱一下。

Annie: Okay. Go ahead and I'll be around here. Just call me if you get lost.

安妮：好啊，去吧，我會在這附近。如果你迷路的話可以打給我。

Bell: By the way, are there bats here?

貝兒：對了，這裡有蝙蝠嗎？

 三問三答　*MP3 06*

01
Question

What are some of the most interesting caves in the world?
世界上有哪一些有趣的洞穴呢？

Michelle
蜜雪兒

Have you heard about the Cave of Crystals in Mexico?

33

Doesn't it just sound so fascinating? I randomly read about it on a magazine, while I was getting a haircut, and I have been really interested about going to see it. It's said that the crystal formation in that cave is huge. It is over 9 meters long and 1 meter wide. I really want to see this giant crystal, but I heard it's disturbingly hot in that cave. Well...no wonder the crystal is still there...

你有聽過墨西哥的巨型水晶洞穴嗎？你不覺得聽起來就很吸引人嗎？我有一次在剪頭髮的時候不小心在雜誌上看到的，然後我就一直想去看。聽說在洞穴裡的水晶體十分巨大。大概有九公尺高，然後一公尺寬。我是真的很想去看這個巨型水晶，但是我聽說在洞穴裡是超級熱的。哎…難怪那些水晶都還在那…

Matt
麥特

There is an interesting cave in the island of Capri in Italy. It's interesting because there's an eerie blue light in the cave. I went to that cave in the afternoon, which was a really good time to visit because that was the time when the sunlight was filtered through seawater and created a blue reflection. It was phenomenal to see. I took so many pictures there.

　　在義大利卡布里島有一個很有趣的洞穴。它很有趣是因為它洞穴裡有一道很詭異的藍光。我去的時候是在下午，聽說那是一個很好的時機，因為那時候陽光會透過海水照進洞穴，然後就會產生反射的藍光。真的是很壯觀。我在那拍了超多照片的。

Becca
貝卡

When I was doing the Working Holiday in New Zealand, I went to Aranui cave that is known for its glowworms. Glowworms are very much like fireflies but they are different from each other. It's a must see in that area. When I went in the cave on a boat ride, there were thousands of glowworms illuminating. That was the most beautiful scene I've ever seen.

　　我在紐西蘭度假打工的時候有去一個以螢火蟲聞名的阿拉努伊洞穴。在洞穴裡的這種螢火蟲跟一般的螢火蟲不太一樣。在那個區域是必看的。我坐船去那個洞穴看的時候，那裡有上千隻螢火蟲在發光。那是我目前為止看過最美的景象。

| 02 Question | What kind of equipment do you think you need to explore caves? 你覺得探索洞穴的時候需要哪一些配備呢？ |

Michelle
蜜雪兒

Speaking from my past experiences, I definitely need to bring clothes that I don't care about. It is just so wet and muddy in the caves. I ruined a white T-shirt and my brand name shoes the last time I was in a cave. I was very upset. So, boots and towels to dry off as well. I don't have to be a cavewoman when I go to a cave, right?

這是我的經驗談， 我一定要帶我不在意的衣服。因為洞穴裡真的又濕又泥濘。我有一次去洞穴裡的時候就毀了我一件白色 T 恤和一雙名牌的鞋子。我那時候真的很不爽。所以囉，靴子，還有要擦乾的毛巾。我去洞穴不代表我就要變成一個野蠻人對吧？

Matt
麥特

I've heard a lot of stories when people got stuck in the caves. So, I think for me, I would want to bring extra food and water. Ropes and warm clothes to prepare for the worst. I might sound paranoid, but better safe than sorry, right?

我有聽過很多人被困在洞穴裡的故事。所以我想對我來說，我會要帶多點的食物和水，繩子還有保暖的衣服來作最壞的打算。我聽起來好像有點神經質，可是安全一點總比之後遺憾還要好吧？

Becca
貝卡

Of course you need to bring a helmet, flashlight, and extra lights actually just in case. A raincoat would come in handy when you go exploring the caves. You have to watch out for some cave creatures, so you might want to bring a company. It can be kind of creepy walking in the caves.

當然你會需要安全帽、手電筒，還有額外的燈以防萬一。有雨衣的話，在你去探索洞穴的時候也是很方便的。還要小心一些洞穴裡的生物，所以帶個夥伴也是一個好主意。走在洞穴裡的時候其實還蠻令人毛骨悚然的。

03 Question

What are some of the stories you have heard about caves?
你有聽過關於洞穴的什麼故事嗎？

Michelle
蜜雪兒

I saw the animation called The Croods a while back ago. It was a really cute story. The Croods are the last group of cavemen on earth, and they believe that they cannot leave the cave once it's dark. It's their only safe place when the darkness comes until one day they started their adventure outside of the cave and pursued after the sun. It's a really funny and sweet story.

我前陣子有看了一部動畫叫做古魯家族。那是一個很可愛的故事。古魯家族是世界上唯一剩下的野人。他們相信他們天黑之後就一定不能離開洞穴。天黑之後他們唯一安全的地方就是洞穴裡。直到有一天他們開始了在洞穴外面追逐著太陽的冒險。那是一個很好笑又很窩心的電影。

Matt
麥特

The only thing I can think of is Bat Man. The cave is where Bat Man stores all his undercover life. That's always my favorite part when the Bat Man drives his car out of the cave, and the bats fly with him.

我唯一想到的就是蝙蝠俠。蝙蝠俠就是在洞穴裡面儲藏他所有的臥底生活。我最喜歡的一部分就是當蝙蝠俠開車飛出洞穴的時候，很多蝙蝠跟著他飛起的那幕。

Becca
貝卡

Everyone knows about Plato's allegory of the cave! A bunch of people grew up in a cave, and when one of them got out of the cave, he had a hard time getting used to the

sunlight, but then he saw the beauty of the world, and decided to go back and told his people about it. Everyone thought he was crazy and killed him. It's crazy what people would do to stay in their comfort zone.

大家都知道柏拉圖的洞穴的寓言。有一群人是在洞穴裡面長大的，然後當他們其中一個人走出了洞穴，他很難適應陽光，但是當他適應了之後，他看見了這個世界有多美，他決定會回去告訴其他人。但是大家都以為他瘋了要帶他們出洞穴，於是他們就把他殺了。大家為了要待在舒適圈裡而做出來的事真的是很誇張。

 Useful expressions

⛵ **mind blowing** 令人震撼的

❶ The amount of work he's doing is mind blowing.

他的工作量真的真很令人震撼。

⛵ **heads up** 提醒，提點

❷ Thanks for the heads up the other day. I did well at the interview.

謝謝你那天的提點。我面試的很順利。

⛵ **drama queen** 戲劇化，小題大作的人

❸ Quit being the drama queen. It's just a cockroach.

不要那麼誇張啦！只是一隻蟑螂而已！

⛵ speaking from one's experience 某人的經驗談

❹ He's speaking from his own experience, he took the test 3 times.

他是在講自己的經驗談，他那個考試考了三次。

⛵ prepare for the worst 做最壞的打算

❺ I always hope for the best and prepare for the worst.

我總是最樂觀的希望但是做好最壞的打算。

⛵ better safe than sorry 安全勝過遺憾

❻ Buckle up the seat belts. It's better safe than sorry.

繫好安全帶！安全勝過遺憾啊！

洞穴

⛵ come in handy 派上用途

❼ Just bring your umbrella with you. It might come in handy. It's pretty cloudy outside.

你就帶著你的雨傘啦。今天可能會派上用途。今天還蠻多雲的。

⛵ comfort zone 舒適圈

❽ It is very hard to step out of the comfort zone, but we shall try.

要踏出舒適圈是很不容易的事，但是我們還是要試試看。

National Park
國家公園

4

Unit

 背景起源

Few scenes on Earth are as awe-inspiring as gazing over the vast mountains, and the colors of the National Parks. Yet it is only small parts of the National Parks. There is so much magnificence to be found across the countries. Parks offer everything from wonderful hiking trails, photography and wildlife viewing opportunities, to stargazing or even boating. There is so much to do at any one of the parks, and it's a fantastic way to spend time with the family. National Parks are great for all ages. It's educational and most of all, and the serenity of parks makes for a very relaxing experience. Ready or not, the adventure is out there and within the National Park!

　　在地球上很少地方可以像國家公園裡那廣闊的山峽和美麗的顏色一樣令人驚艷。但是這只是國家公園的一小部份。在每個國家都有很多的美景。國家公園提供了從健行步道，攝影和野生動物觀賞景點到觀星還有航行的機會。在國家公園裡面可以做的事情很多，而在那也是和家人共渡美好時光的地方。每個年齡層都很適合去國家公園，國家公園十分具教育性，而且最重要的是國家公園裡的寧靜可以提供一個十分令人放鬆的經驗。不管你準備好了沒有，冒險都是在戶外，或是在國家公園裡！

Dialogue 情境對話 MP3 07

Christie and Ben are going glamping at the Yellowstone National Park.
克里斯婷和班正要去黃石公園裡豪華露營。

Ben: What exactly is glamping anyways?

班：豪華露營到底是什麼啊？

Christie: Glamping is a blended word for glamorous camping. That's something I knew existed, but I had never tried before. But here we are!!

克里斯婷：豪華露營就是豪華的露營方式的混合字啦！我以前就知道有這個東西可是從來沒有試過。但現在我們在這啦！

Ben: Glamorous camping? Sounds very girly.

班：豪華的是露營方式？聽起來好娘喔。

國家公園

Christie: Okay relax Mr. Boy Scout. It's something different, and I just want to see what it is.

克里斯婷：欸放輕鬆一點，童子軍。我只是想要試試看不一樣的東西。

Ben: What happens to real camping or staying in a hotel?

班：幹嘛不真正的露營還是住在飯店就好了？

Christie: It's actually their <u>high season</u> right now, so they were all booked out. This was our only option, and frankly, I'm really excited to see what they have to offer.

克里斯婷：因為現在是旺季，他們都被訂光了。這是唯一還可以訂的，而且老實說，我真的還蠻期待看看他們有什麼好玩的。

Ben: Oh I see, thanks for arranging everything Christie. Yeah, this is going to be the first paid camping trip for me! That would be something new.

班：喔，我了解了。謝謝你安排這些阿克里斯婷。嗯，這會是我第一個要付錢的露營經驗！會是全新的體驗。

Christie: Quit being so negative. We're about to have a tent with a king-size bed, a dresser and wood-burning stove. It's going to be fun!

克里斯婷：不要那麼負面嘛。我們會有一個特大號的床，一個衣櫃，還有一個木頭火爐。一定會很好玩的！

Ben: Oh wow, how much is it a night?

班：喔哇，一個晚上多少啊？

Christie: 150 dollars. Hold on, Ben, before you say anything, can I just say that all the reviews about glamping at this place are all great.

克里斯婷：一百五十塊美金。等下，班，在你說話之前，我只想說所有對這裡豪華露營的評價都很高分。

Ben: I wasn't going to say anything bad! I'm getting excited about this. Camping without doing all the work. Bravo to that!

班：我又沒有要說什麼不好的！我越來越期待了。不用做任何苦功的露營！太棒啦！

國家公園

01
Question

Have you ever been to any National parks?
If not, which one do you want to visit?

你有去過國家公園嗎？沒有的話，你想要去哪一個國家公園呢？

Michelle
蜜雪兒

I've been to several National parks in the world, but I would tell you that Jiuahaigou Vally National Park in China is just magical. The five-colored lakes, the clear sky and the evergreen forests are just amazing on its own. <u>Heaven on earth</u> would be the best description for it.

我有去過全世界很多座國家公園，但是我覺得最夢幻的是中國的九寨溝國家公園。五色沼、晴朗的天空和常青的森林分開看就已經很美了。對它最好的描述就是人間天堂。

Matt
麥特

I've been to Arenal National Park in Costa Rica. I heard many movies were shot in that National park. I have no doubts about it. It's just so lush and there is an active volcano within the national park! How cool is that! Because of the volcano, there are plenty of hot springs as well. If you talk to the locals, they will take you to the hidden waterfalls, too!

我有去過哥斯大黎加的 Arenal 國家公園。我聽說很多電影在那裡拍攝過。我完全沒有疑問。那裡真的很翠綠，而且還有一個活火山在國家公園裡。超酷的！因為有火山，那裡也有很多的溫泉。如果你跟當地人聊天認識的話，他們還會帶你去秘密瀑布呢！

國家公園

Becca
貝卡

Yes, I've been to Yosemite National Park. The view there is just breathtaking. I went in spring and that was when all the wildflowers were in bloom. Besides, the crystalline lakes and the pine forests just make perfect postcard-worthy

views all around you!

　　有啊，我有去過優勝美地國家公園。那裡的景色真的美不勝收。我是春天的時候去的，在那個時候所有的野花都盛開。除此之外，清澈的湖水和松樹森林讓你周遭的景色都好像明信片一樣。

02
Question

What are the things you expect to see or do in the National Parks?
你預期在國家公園可以看到什麼或是做什麼呢？

Michelle
蜜雪兒

I expect to join the guided tour in the National Parks. I cannot stress enough the importance of letting people who know what they are doing show you around in their playground. Horseback riding tours, or some private tours would be ideal.

　　我預期可以參加國家公園裡的導覽。我沒辦法強調讓知道該做什麼的人帶你去他們的地盤參觀的重要性。騎馬行程，或是一些私人行程都很理想。

Matt
麥特

I expect to see a lot of wildlife in the National Parks for sure. Some National Parks even give out maps of where to see those animals. Bear, bighorn sheep, bison, elk, and river otters all wander in the parks. I was once really close to a bear. It was frightening, but also amazing to see a bear in such a short distance. I was in awe to see such a beautiful creature in the National Parks and I would love to see more of them.

我一定是預期在國家公園裡看到很多野生動物。有一些國家公園甚至會給你一個地圖去看動物。熊、大角羊、美洲野牛、麋鹿和水獺都在公園裡到處遊蕩。我有一次很接近一隻熊。其實蠻恐怖的，但是同時也是很神奇可以這麼近看著熊。我那時候看到這麼美的生物真的很震撼，我還想要再看多一些。

Becca
貝卡

I've always imagined the stars are all over the place in

國家公園

the National Parks, the forests and <u>all that jazz</u>. Avatar is what I have in mind when it comes to the National Parks. I also want to do some hiking and camping when I'm in a National Park I think.

我總是想像在國家公園裡到處都是星星、森林諸如此類的。想到國家公園我就會想到阿凡達。我也想要在國家公園裡健行或是露營。

03 Question
What do you think is the purpose of the National Parks?
你覺得國家公園的目的是什麼？

Michelle
蜜雪兒

Off the record, I think the real purpose of the National Parks is to attract more tourists and make money out of it. Think about it, the land has always been there, and the government claims the land and builds a park on it. What is the difference between a National Park and an entertainment park?

　　私下跟你說，我覺得國家公園真正的目的只是要吸引遊客來賺多一點錢。你想想看，土地本來就在那裡，國家徵收那個土地，然後在上面蓋了個公園。那國家公園跟遊樂園有什麼不一樣？

Matt
麥特

　　I was volunteering at the Yellowstone National Park for a while. The purpose of the National Park is to preserve and protect the natural resources for the future generation. We really do a lot to help preserve the beauty of the park. Places like that should be well preserved so that more people can see them in the future.

　　我有在黃石國家公園當了一陣子的志工。國家公園的目的是在於為了下一代保存，還有保護國家資源。我們在園區內真的做了很多保護美景的工作。這麼美麗的地方應該要被好好的保存下來給未來更多的人看到。

Becca
貝卡

I think besides the obvious reason to preserve the place, most National Parks are trying to educate people about the place. They often provide opportunities for people to experience and understand the wildlife and the environment. I think it's a classroom where the real education happens.

我想除了很明顯的保存那個地方之外，大多數的國家公園也都試著要宣導那個國家公園。他們也會有讓人們體驗或瞭解野生動物或是環境的機會。我覺得國家公園是一個教育真的發生的教室。

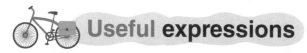 **Useful expressions**

⚓ **stargazing** 觀星

❶ What is the best stargazing site here?

這裡最棒的觀星點在哪裡啊？

⚓ **ready or not** 不管你準備好了沒有

❷ Ready or not, we're going to graduate soon!

不管你準備好了沒有，我們很快就要畢業了！

⚓ **glamping** 豪華露營

❸ I'm really excited about our upcoming glamping trip! We are going to stay in a tree house!

我超期待我們接下來要去的豪華露營！我們要住在樹屋裡面耶！

⚓ **high season** 旺季

❹ We have to book our tickets soon. June is the high season, so it's going to be more and more expensive.

我們要趕快訂我們的票了。六月是旺季，所以票會越來越貴喔！

⚓ **heaven on earth** 人間天堂

❺ I heard Maldives is truly heaven on earth. We should go there for our honeymoon!

我聽說馬爾地夫真的是人間天堂。我們應該要去那裡度蜜月！

⚓ **cannot stress enough** 強調非常重要

❻ I cannot stress enough about the importance of eating healthy! You can't do anything without health.

我無法強調吃得健康有多麼重要！沒有健康你什麼也做不了。

⚓ **all that jazz** 諸如此類的

❼ He only cares about basketball, girls and all that jazz.

他只關心籃球、女生那類的。

國家公園

⑤ Canyon
大峽谷

Unit

 背景起源

One of the best ways to peek at nature's wonders is to pay a visit to the canyons. Although there is just one that was named as such, the earth is home to many grand canyons. From very steep cliffs to extremely narrow valleys, each reveals a sense of wonder and magnificence while documenting thousands of years of geological history. Although each is unique in its own way, there are still must-sees for any nature lover. But be aware, if you have a fear of heights, you may feel uncomfortable just gazing down at the canyon, or if you don't have enough gigabytes for your memory cards, you might be taking a lot of pictures. Canyon is a scenic wonder that attracts travelers with its numerous trails for both the experienced and inexperienced hikers. Come check out the amazing things our planet has to offer!

要窺視大自然奇景最棒的方法之一就是去看一些峽谷！雖然只有一

個峽谷是命名為大峽谷，地球上還有很多其他的大峽谷！從很陡峭的懸崖到很窄的峽谷，每一個都透露出自然的奇景和雄偉，同一時候它也為幾千年的地質歷史做下了紀錄。雖然每一個峽谷都有它特別的地方，還是有很多是大自然愛好者必去的地方。但小心！如果你怕高的話，你可能從狹谷看下去的時候會很害怕，或是你的記憶卡可能會因為你可能會拍很多照片而容量不足。峽谷是一個用很多步道吸引遊客的美麗景點。步道有適合比較有經驗的登山客，也有給比較沒有經驗的人。快來看看我們這個星球還有什麼很棒的景觀吧！

 ## Dialogue 情境對話 MP3 09

Eddie and Betty are at the Waimea Canyon in Kauai.
艾迪和貝蒂正在可愛島的懷梅阿峽谷。

Betty: This is the most colorful canyon I've ever seen! So red, and green, and yellow...

貝蒂：這真是我看過最多顏色的峽谷！那麼紅色、綠色還有黃色…

Eddie: Yeah, it's beautiful. Isn't this where the movie "The Descendants" was shot? You know the one starred George Clooney?

艾迪：對啊，真的好漂亮喔。這不是"繼承人生"拍片的地方嗎？你知道就是喬治克隆尼主演的那片？

Betty: Oh that's right. No wonder this

貝蒂：喔對喔！難怪我

place looks a little familiar! I knew I have seen this from somewhere. For a moment I thought I was having a <u>Déjà vu</u>! That's what it is!

Eddie: Yeah, it took me a while, too. Can you imagine actors get to travel to beautiful places like this to work, and then they get millions of dollars?

Betty: Sounds like a <u>sweet deal</u> to me! Too bad we're no Julia Roberts or Angelina Jolie!

Eddie: I know, right. Hey! Look at those goats in the canyon! How did they get there?

Betty: Oh wow, they must have very good balance, considering they have to walk on those little heels.

覺得這個地方有點眼熟。我就知道我有在哪裡看過這個地方。我就覺得似曾相識！就是那部片啦！

艾迪：對啊，我也想了一下。你可以想像那些演員可以到這麼美的地方工作，然後他們就賺了幾百萬？

貝蒂：聽起來好棒喔！真可惜我們不是茉莉亞羅柏茲還是安潔麗娜裘利！

艾迪：我知道。欸，你看那些在峽谷裡的山岩！他們怎麼到那裡的？

貝蒂：喔哇！他們的平衡一定很好，而且他們還有了那些小小的跟。

Eddie: Hahaha...yeah, there are a few trails around the canyon, should we give them a try?

艾迪：哈哈哈…對啊，欸這裡有一些步道耶，我們要不要去試試看？

Betty: Yeah sure, I'm up to whatever!

貝蒂：好啊，我什麼都可以！

Eddie: The red dirt here is just amazing! It's so red!

艾迪：那些紅土真的很驚人耶！好紅喔！

Betty: It definitely adds the characters to this place!

貝蒂：真的為這個地方多添了一點特色。

Eddie: I'm gonna scoop some dirt home for souvenir...

艾迪：我要挖一些土回家當紀念品…

大峽谷

01 Question

Have you ever been to any canyon?

你有曾經去過任何峽谷嗎？

Michelle
蜜雪兒

Canyon? Me? No way! Do you know how many accidents happened at the canyons? People fall in there all the time. Alright, I might be a little dramatic, but you get the point. And who knows, what if it rains, there might be falling rocks! I certainly do not want to wear helmets when I'm traveling. I travel with styles. Period.

峽谷？我嗎？不可能的！你知道在峽谷有多少意外發生過嗎？大家一天到晚都掉到峽谷裡。好啦，我是有點誇張，可是你知道我的意思。而且誰知道啊，如果下雨的話，還可能會有落石耶！我真的不想要戴安全帽旅行。我要很時尚的旅行。就是這樣。

Matt
麥特

Yes, certainly. That's one of the must-sees for me. I went to Grand Canyon a few years ago, and it didn't disappoint me in any way! It's just as grand as I imagined. I feel so teeny when I was there. It's definitely a place that humbles you. The Native Americans consider this place as a holy place, and I can see that.

有啊，當然。那是我必去的地方之一。我幾年前有去過大峽谷，而且他也完全沒有令我失望！那就跟我想像的一樣那麼大！我在那裡的時候覺得我好小喔。那個地方真的會讓你覺得很謙卑。那裡同時也是印第安人覺得是很神聖的地方，我看得出來。

大峽谷

Becca
貝卡

I was traveling in Tibet, and had a chance to visit the Yurlung Tsangpo Canyon. They claimed that it was the highest river in the world, and that's why the name of the canyon meant "The Everest of Rivers". It is a place that's

really close to heaven I think. Very pure and clean.

我有去西藏玩然後去了雅魯藏波峽谷。他們號稱那裡是世界上最高的河流。那也是它名字的意思。意思是說那是河流裡的聖母峰。而且我也覺得那裡是最接近天堂的地方。非常的純淨跟乾淨。

02 Question

Why do you think canyons are so popular?
你覺得為什麼峽谷很受歡迎呢？

Michelle
蜜雪兒

Honestly I have no clue. I guess people would say something about the wonder of the nature blah-blah-blah, but what about safety? What happens to treasuring your own precious life? Many people went missing in the canyons, and I can imagine where they went.

老實說我真的不懂耶。我想大家可能會說因為那是大自然的奇景啊這類無聊的話，但是安全怎麼辦？要怎麼保護我們寶貴的生命呢？很多人在峽谷裡失蹤，我可以想像他們是去了哪裡。

I don't know. I like it because it's just a great reminder to stay humble, and <u>it's only natural to</u> be drawn to something so grand. Not to mention that none of it is man-made. It's all from our mother earth. We only live at small parts on this planet, and I can't wait and I know for sure that more wonders will be discovered in the future.

我不知道耶。我喜歡是因為那是可以提醒我保持謙卑的地方，而且我覺得是很自然而然被這麼巨大的地方吸引。更別提它完全不是人造的。完全是來自我們的大地之母。我們只住在這個星球上很小的一部分，我等不及要看，而且我確定有更多的奇景在這個世界上等著被探索。

大峽谷

Well...it's mostly because we heard these places during the geography class when we were growing up. You know the name, and then you started watching Discovery or

National Geographic channel. It's one of the most amazing things, and it must be true because the textbooks and Discovery and National Geographic don't lie. The next thing you know, you're posting a picture on Facebook of you and the canyon.

　　嗯…我想大多是因為我們以前在上地理課的時候就有聽過這些地方，你就知道那些名字。然後你就開始看探索或是國家地理頻道。那是世界上最驚人的事物之一，而且也一定是真的，因為課本、探索，還有國家地理頻道不會騙人。然後你就發現你正在臉書上 po 一張你跟峽谷的照片。

03
Question

Have you heard about the zip lining across the canyon?
你有聽過可以高空滑索過峽谷嗎？

Michelle
蜜雪兒

　　Oh my gosh, this is just <u>getting out of the hand</u>! First, they want people to go to the canyon with chances that they might fall to death, and now they take a step further to actually hang them in the mid air in the canyon? Bravo! What do they just stab them at the back? That's faster.

我的天啊！這越來越無法收拾了！首先他們要大家冒著可能會摔死的生命危險去峽谷，然後他們又更進一步的要把大家吊在峽谷的空中？做得好！他們幹嘛不要就從大家的背後捅一刀就好了？那樣比較快。

Matt
麥特

Yep, I actually did that when I was at the Grand Canyon. It was really exciting and super fun. It's a view you can't beat unless you are in the helicopter. The canyon was super deep, so I had a few nerve breakdowns when the ride got rough, but I would totally do it again! It was really fun!

有啊，其實我在大峽谷就有去玩。真的很刺激又超級好玩的。除非你坐直升機進去不然那個景觀是無法打敗的。峽谷很深所以當滑索變得有點不順的時候我其實還蠻緊張的，但是我一定會再去一次的！真的超級好玩的！

Becca
貝卡

What?! The textbook didn't say that! That sounds like fun! I would love to try it one day. Can you imagine? We usually just stay behind the bars when we are at the canyon. Wait, is this just a hypothetical question or there actually is zip lining at the canyons?

什麼？！課本沒有說啊！聽起來蠻好玩的！我有一天一定要試試看。你能想像嗎？我們通常去峽谷的時候都要站在欄杆後面。等下，這是一個假設的問題還是峽谷真的有高空滑索？

 **Useful expressions**

⚓ **Déjà vu 似曾相識的**

❶ I just had a Déjà vu when I was there. It was so weird!

我剛剛在那個地方一直覺得我好像有去過那裡。真的好奇怪喔。

⚓ **sweet deal 順心的交易，很棒的交易**

❷ That was such a sweet deal! You should take the job!

那是很棒的條件耶！你應該要接受那個工作的！

⚓ **up to whatever** 什麼都可以

❸ I am up to whatever you guys want to do!

你們要做什麼我都可以阿！

⚓ **add the characters to** 為…增添特色

❹ The scars just add the characters to my leg.

這些疤為我的腳增添特色。

⚓ **period** 句點，就是這樣

❺ I am not going. Period.

我是不會去的。就是這樣。

⚓ **blah-blah-blah** 無聊的話，廢話

❻ He just kept on talking about politics and blah-blah-blah. You know how he is.

他就一直聊政治還有那類無聊的話。你知道他就是那樣。

⚓ **It's only natural to** 很自然的

❼ It's only natural to worry about your children. Don't worry, they are usually fine.

擔心你的孩子是很自然的。別擔心啦，他們通常都會沒事。

⚓ **getting out of hand** 失去控制

❽ This is getting out of hand. I don't know what to do to keep everyone in line.

這已快失去我能控制的範圍了。我不知道該怎麼讓大家規矩一點！

6 Sunrise 日出

Unit

 背景起源

Kicking back on the beach, a cold beer in hand while watching the sun go down is one of the many travelers' pleasures. But there's something way more rewarding about dragging yourself from bed in the pitch black and half-sleepingly hiking to the top of a mountain or the edge of a cliff to see the sun rise in all its glory on a good day. You'll have the whole day stretching out ahead of you, and full of amazing adventures to be had. Or, if you are feeling snoozy, you can always go back to bed to take a well-deserved nap afterwards. Head to one of these amazing spots and be ready to be dazzled!

放鬆地坐在海邊，一邊享受著手中的冰啤酒，一邊看著夕陽西下是很多旅行者最享受的事情之一。但是在一個好日子，當天還是黑漆漆的時候，就把你自己從床上拖起來，然後在半睡半醒間健行到山頂，或是懸崖的一角，看太陽榮耀的升起，是比看夕陽還要更有價值的。你看完之後還有一整天在你眼前，以及很多冒險等著你。或者是如果你覺得想睡覺，你可以回去睡一個你應得的午覺。去最棒的地方看日出，然後你可能會因為日出的美而覺得眼花撩亂！

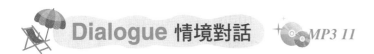

Dialogue 情境對話　　MP3 11

James and Vivian are about to watch sunrise at Ali Mountain.
詹姆士和微微安正要去阿里山看日出。

James: Vivian wake up! I made you a cup of coffee! Time to wake up and get ready to go!

詹姆士：微微安！起床了！我幫你泡了一杯咖啡！該起來了我們該走了！

Vivian: I didn't sleep too well. I couldn't fall asleep all night.

微微安：我昨天沒睡好。我昨天晚上都睡不著。

James: Aw, we'll take a nap when we come back! Now it's time to go! We came here for the sunrise!

詹姆士：喔，我們回來的時候可以睡個午覺！現在該走了！我們來這就是要看日出的啊！

Vivian: What time is sunrise? Maybe I can sleep for another half an hour?

微微安：日出是幾點啊？搞不好我還可以再睡個半小時？

日出

James: We went through all this yesterday. We have to leave here in 15 minutes!

詹姆士：我們昨天就想好了。我們必須在十五分鐘後就要出發！

Vivian: Perfect, I'll sleep for 5 more minutes. I don't need anything, so I can get ready really quickly.

微微安：太好了，那我再睡五分鐘。我不用準備什麼所以我很快就可以出發了。

James: Okay, but we don't want to miss the train, and if you still want breakfast...

詹姆士：好啦，但是我們不能錯過火車，而且如果你還想要吃早餐的話…

Vivian: Alright, I'm awake. This sunrise is better be good.

微微安：好啦，我醒了啦。這個日出最好很好看。

(When they are at the top of the mountain)

（當他們登頂的時候）

Vivian: Look at the cloud. It's like ocean up here with all the colorful waves.

微微安：你看那個雲！在這裡好像是有彩色的浪的海喔。

James: You're exactly right. They call

詹姆士：你講得很對。

it sea of cloud here. It's really breathtaking. Aren't you glad you woke up?

他們這裡就叫它雲海。真的很美吧。你現在有沒有很高興你有醒來？

Vivian: Sorry, I was being a drag. I was still sleeping I think.

微微安：對不起我早上一直拖。我那時候應該還在睡覺。

James: No problem. We made it. That's the important part!

詹姆士：沒問題啦。我們到啦。那是最重要的！

Vivian: Now what? Should we explore a little around here since we're here?

微微安：那現在我們要幹嘛？既然都來了我們要不要就去到處探索一下？

James: It's my turn to get a little tired...

詹姆士：換我有點累了…

01 Question

Do you like watching sunrise? Why or why not?

你喜歡看日出嗎？為什麼會是為什麼不喜歡？

Michelle
蜜雪兒

Sunrise is beautiful but not beautiful enough for me to sacrifice my beauty sleep. Waking up in the midnight just so that I can catch the sunrise for a little bit. And guess what? Sometimes you do all that in vain!! In vain! The best people can tell you is that "Oh, it's not the best day to watch sunrise today." What?! Excuse me, all that waking up at midnight, hiking and all the fuss end up with nothing? What's wrong with stargazing, moonrise or those activities that take less effort?

日出是很漂亮，可是沒有漂亮到讓我想要犧牲我的美容覺。要大半夜起床所以我才可以看到日出一下下。然後你知道怎樣嗎？有的時候你所做的一切都是白費的！白費的耶！然後別人只能說：「啊今天不是很適合看日出！」什麼？不好意思你說什麼？所以半夜起床，然後爬山到山頂還有所有做的麻煩事到頭來什麼都看不到？觀星、看月亮升起，還有那些不用那麼辛苦的行程有什麼不好的？

Matt
麥特

Yes, who doesn't love sunrise? You wake up early when it is still dark, you <u>bundle yourself up</u> and hike the highest point so that you can peek at the best view of something that secretly happens every day. It just makes me feel the view is that much better when you go through all that effort. The colors of the cloud and the moment when sun shows up at the horizon just makes me feel that all that work is worthwhile. Here's the beautiful start of my day!

喜歡啊，誰不喜歡日出？你早上在天還是黑黑的時候起來，把你自己包滿了保暖的衣服，然後爬到最高的點，你就可以窺視到這個其實每天都偷偷在發生的美景。我覺得那麼辛苦才看到的日出更好看。雲的顏色，還有當太陽出現在地平線的那一刻，就讓我覺得這一切都是值得的。美好的一天就要開始了！

日出

Becca
貝卡

I do really like sunrise. There is something magical and holy about it. Many people go all the way to the mountain just to bid their good morning to the sun. It's really something to see up there. However, in exchange, you have to wake up so early that you might as well just stay up late. I drank so much coffee that I was shaking.

我真的喜歡日出。我覺得他有一種很神奇跟神聖的感覺。很多人爬上去就只是為了要跟太陽說早安。上去之後看到的美景真的蠻棒的。但是，要看到這美景，你就得要很早起床。早到你乾脆熬夜不要睡好了。我那時候喝超多咖啡喝到我都發抖了。

02
Question

Where have you seen the most beautiful sunrise?
你在哪裡看過最美的日出？

Michelle
蜜雪兒

Sunrise? Of course at Mountain Ali in Taiwan! Where else do you go? When I was there, I had to <u>lower myself to everyone's level</u> to get in the tiny train for getting up to the mountain. I'd always imagined that we'd get in a luxurious chariot at 3 or 4 in the morning and just wave around the sparklers. So dreamy, and then some servers would have the delicious food ready on the side when you were enjoying the sunrise. I guess they didn't <u>live up to my expectation</u> at all!

看曙光？當然是要去阿里山啊？不然你覺得還有什麼地方好去？想當初我去看的時候可是勉強搭乘小火車上去？我一直覺得該乘坐豪華馬車零晨三四點左右，乘著馬車邊拿著仙女棒朝著天空劃呀劃的。蠻夢幻的。然後隨從們還準備好美食，在看曙光時享用。我想他們一點也沒有我預期的那麼好。

Matt
麥特

I went to Haleakala in the Island of Maui. My friends and I got up at 3 so that the traffic to the mountain wasn't too bad. We made it to the top, and quickly found out it was freezing there. Luckily we brought a lot of extra blankets in the car. When the sun was about to rise, the colors of the cloud changed so quickly that I had no choice but to keep taking a lot of pictures. When the sun rose, everyone was in awe of the scene in front of us.

我去茂伊島的哈來阿卡拉。我的朋友跟我三點就起床了所以比較不會塞車。我們登頂的時候很快就發現山上超冷的。好險我們車子裡有多帶一些毯子。當太陽快要升起的時候，雲的顏色一直很快的變化所以我只好一直拍。當太陽真的升起的時候，大家都對眼前的景色感到震驚。

Becca
貝卡

I watched the sunrise at Fiji. It was during the New Year's Eve actually. My friends and I decided that we wanted to catch one of the first sunrises in the world to welcome the upcoming New Year, so we went to Fiji and it was very nice. We completed our first of the year by scuba diving afterwards as well!

　我在斐濟看日出。那時候其實是跨年夜。我的朋友和我想要看到世界上最早出來的日出來歡迎新的一年，所以我們就去斐濟，然後也真的蠻棒的。我們看完日落之後就去深潛來讓這新年的第一天更完美。

03
Question

Do you prefer sunrise or sunset? Why?
你比較喜歡日出還是日落呢？為什麼？

Michelle
蜜雪兒

　Sunset, sunset, and sunset for sure! Duh! Tell me one thing that sunrise is better than sunset. You can't. Because they are equally amazing, but sunset is right there for you to enjoy without any painstaking hiking, or waking up at midnight. You just enjoy the sunset from whichever spot you wish and have a glass of cocktail. Who says you always

日出

have to work so hard for amazing things?

日落、日落，一定是日落的阿！還要說嘛！你跟我說一個日出比日落好的地方。你不行。因為他們其實真的一樣棒，可是日落你不用很辛苦的爬山還是早起，它就在你眼前。你可以在任何你喜歡的地方看夕陽，然後再來杯調酒。誰說你一定要很辛苦才可以得到美好的事物？

I prefer sunrise. Sunrise is more like an award for those who are willing to get up and hike in the early morning. That just makes it and me feel so much more special. People won't be amazed when you tell them you just watch the sunset, but they will when you watch the sunrise. It's a bit shallow I know, but I love it. I feel like I accomplish something every time I watch the sunrise.

我比較喜歡日出。日出其實對我來說比較像是可以早起的人的獎項。那麼辛苦只會讓我覺得日出更加的特別。如果你跟他們說你看了日落，大家不會覺得你很厲害，但是如果說你看了日出，他們會覺得你很厲害。有點膚淺我知道啦，可是我就是很喜歡嘛。我每次看完日出就覺得我好像完成了什麼。

Becca
貝卡

Woo...that's a tough one. They are both so beautiful. However, I guess I prefer sunrise. It is just something that I would want to join a group of friends and plan together to do. Whereas, sunset is more casual and you can't really plan a trip out of it. With sunrise, we probably have to travel to stay at the hotel near the spot the night before, wake up early and hike up. It's just a more complete trip and I prefer that.

哇…這題蠻難的。他們都那麼美。但是我想我應該會選日出。因為看日出是我會想要跟一群朋友一起計劃要做的事。但是我覺得日落是比較隨性的。而且你也不能真的安排出一個看日落的行程。看日出的話，我們可能要前一天晚上就要住在附近的旅社，早起，然後爬上去看日出。看日出就是一個比較完整的行程啊，而且我也比較喜歡那樣啦。

 Useful expressions

日出

▲ **kick back 放輕鬆**

❶ We have some refreshments and drinks on the side, so everyone can just kick back and enjoy the presentation.

我們在旁邊有一些小點心跟飲料，所以大家可以放輕鬆然後聽我們的簡報。

77

⚓ **pitch dark** 漆黑的

❷ When we were walking in the woods, it was pitch dark, and we were all very scared.

當我們走在森林裡的時候，那時候黑漆漆的，而且我們都很害怕。

⚓ **well-deserved** 非常應得的，當之無愧的

❸ After working so hard all week, she went and got a well-deserved massage.

在這麼辛苦的工作了一個禮拜之後，她去做了一個她應得的按摩。

⚓ **drag** 累贅

❹ I wish I were not a drag on my friends when we were hiking.

我希望我們在爬山的時候我不是我朋友的累贅。

⚓ **bundle up** 包起來，穿得很保暖

❺ We'd better bundle up some warm clothes. It's really cold outside.

我們最好多穿一些保暖的衣服。外面真的很冷。

⚓ **lower myself to one's level** 某人放下身段

❻ I don't want to lower my level to Laura's level by gossiping with her.

我不想要跟羅拉一起八卦然後變得跟羅拉一樣的水準。

⛵ live up to someone's expectation 達到某人的期待

❼ I don't think I can ever live up to my dad's expectation. He's never satisfied with me.

我覺得我應該永遠都達不到我爸的期待。他永遠都對我很不滿意。

⛵ that's a tough one 那個蠻難的

❽ I don't understand that question at all. That's a tough one!

我完全不懂那個問題。那題真的蠻難的！

7 Camping
露營

Unit

 背景起源

Have you ever fancied waking up surrounded by nothing but nature and falling asleep under a blanket of stars? It is perhaps one of the best ways to enjoy some <u>quality time</u> with nature. Camping has started to <u>grow on</u> many people through time. Not only do the outdoorsy peeps enjoy this activity, but also folks who are not a big fan of outdoor activities. It has evolved into a more complex system where you may find luxurious camping styles to very down to earth (literally) ones. Whichever fits your needs, it will for sure be a memorable experience and a great opportunity to <u>touch base with</u> nature and your inner adventurous self. As romantic as it sounds, don't forget to check out the rules and possible dangers at your campsite. Pick up your trash after you leave, and leave nothing but your footprints. Be prepared and have fun!

　　你有曾經幻想過在大自然的包圍下醒來，在一片星空下睡著嗎？這或許是和大自然分享親密時光最棒的方法。隨著時間，越來越多人喜歡露營。不只是喜好戶外活動的人，不喜歡戶外的人也漸漸開始喜歡露營。露營已經進化為一個複雜的系統。你可以找到奢華的露營風格，還有非常腳踏實地的（真的跟字面上的意思一樣）不管哪一種比較符合你的需求，露營都一定會給你一個難忘的回憶，而那也是跟大自然以及內在那個冒險的你再次聯繫的好機會。儘管聽起來很浪漫，別忘了查詢相關的露營規則以及營地有可能的危險。而在你離開時只留下你的腳印，而不是垃圾。好好準備，好好玩！

Dialogue 情境對話　　MP3 13

Tammy and Matt are camping on their honeymoon at Hulopo Bay, Lanai Island of Hawaii.
譚咪和麥特正在夏威夷的拉納伊島呼洛柏灣上露營度過他們的蜜月。

Tammy: I don't think I have ever been to such a private beach.	譚咪：我覺得我從來沒有來過這麼隱密的海邊。
Matt: I know what you mean. I would come here all the time if I were someone famous.	麥特：我懂你的意思。如果我很有名的話我一定會常來這。
Tammy: It's so perfect to camp out	譚咪：在這露營真是太

露營

here. Who needs to spend a thousand dollars to stay in the Four Seasons hotel?

完美了。誰需要花幾千美元去待在四季飯店？

Matt: I know, right? They have grills, picnic tables, shower, and you can actually go to the bar at the hotel. I'm sure the five star hotel is nice, but this is my kind of five star accommodation! There are only a few million more stars out here.

麥特：就是說嘛！這裡有烤肉架、野餐桌、沖澡，而且你還可以去飯店內的酒吧。我知道五星級飯店一定很棒，但這是我喜歡的那種五星級住宿！只是外面這有多幾百萬顆星星。

Tammy: That's why I married you.

譚咪：這就是為什麼我會嫁給你。

Matt: Let's set up the tent and then we can go to the grill to fix up our dinner!

麥特：我們來搭帳篷然後去烤肉區準備我們的晚餐吧！

Tammy: I brought steak and asparagus in the cooler!

譚咪：我在小冰箱裡有帶牛排和蘆筍。

Matt: You rock Tammy! I got the blue tooth speaker, so we'll have music, too!

麥特：譚咪你最棒了！我有帶藍牙喇叭，所以我們也有音樂！

Tammy: Hey what's that dolphin sign by the beach?

譚咪：嘿，海邊旁邊的那個海豚的標示牌是什麼？

Matt: Oh, the dolphins come in this bay in the morning, but you're not supposed to swim towards the dolphins because we will disturb them. It is the dolphins' resting ground, too.

麥特：喔，早上的時候海豚會來這個灣，但是你不能朝他們游去因為這樣會打擾到他們。這裡也是海豚休息的地方。

Tammy: Wow, I wish we could swim with the dolphins. That would be so amazing...Oh well...You can't have it all.

譚咪：哇，真希望我們可以跟海豚游泳。那會超棒的…哎，不可能什麼事都稱你的心。

Matt: You know...if we are out there before the dolphins come... Technically, they swim towards us...

麥特：你知道…如果我們在海豚游進來之前就在海裡…說起來的話是他們游向我們…

01 Question

What are some most important things to bring when you go camping?

哪些重要的東西是你露營的時候會帶的？

Michelle
蜜雪兒

Bug repellent is definitely one of the most important things I'll bring. I only use the ones with natural ingredients since I have sensitive skin. I'm born to attract all kinds of bugs. They will <u>eat me alive</u> in the wild. A scar is probably the one souvenir I don't want from the trip. Also, sunscreen is a must when I'm outdoors. Who wants to travel with sunburnt? Not this girl! Oh, and my feather pillow to ensure a good night sleep.

　　驅蟲液一定是我會帶的東西之一。我只用天然成分的驅蟲液因為我是敏感肌膚。我生下來就是會吸引各種的昆蟲。在野外他們會把我生吞掉。旅行的時候我唯一不想帶回來的紀念品就是疤痕。還有，如果我在戶外的話，防曬乳也是一定要的。誰想要邊旅行邊曬傷？不會是我！噢還有我的羽絨枕頭，確保我晚上睡得很好。

Matt
麥特

A water bottle and iodine are always good to have when you need to track down the water source. I bring my fishing pole with me whenever I'm going to be close to the water. It's good to kill time, and you might catch a nutritional dinner. You never know! Most importantly, an open mind is always good since you never know who you are going to run into. I love to talk to people and listen to their stories. An open mind usually leads me to the most amazing experiences.

如果你需要找水源的話，有水壺和碘在身邊的話是很好的。如果我知道我會在水邊露營的話，我也都會帶我的釣竿。那很好殺時間而且說不定你有可能會抓到你的營養晚餐。最重要的是，一個開放的心胸，因為你永遠不知道你會遇到誰。我很喜歡很別人聊天，和聽他們的故事。一個開放的心胸總是帶給我很美好的經驗。

Becca
貝卡

I have this lantern with solar battery. It's called Luci. It's

pretty fantastic. It's light, and lasts for a long time. The bottom line is that the price is so reasonable as well. Also, a spork usually comes in handy when you're eating. A GPS, simple first aid kit... You can never be over prepared.

我有一個太陽能電池的提燈。它叫 Luci。它超棒的。很輕又可以持續很久的時間。最重要的是它的價錢也很合理。還有，匙叉在你吃東西的時候也會很有用！GPS，簡單的急救組…你不可能會準備過頭。

02
Question

What is your best camping experience?
你最棒的露營經驗是什麼呢？

Michelle
蜜雪兒

To be honest, I haven't really camped that many times yet, but I'll say that the time when I was at Uluru was pretty good. I went with the luxurious package where we had Champaign and buffet right in front of Uluru. I cannot imagine anyone who doesn't do this when they finish the day hike there. Oh and did I mention the camel ride before that?

　　老實說，我還沒有露營很多次，但我可以說我在烏魯魯的時候還蠻不錯的。我選了奢華旅行行程。我們在烏魯魯前喝香檳和吃 buffet。我無法想像任何人在健行完之後不選擇這個行程。喔我有提到還有騎駱駝嗎？

Matt
麥特

I had a blast when I was at Jasper National Park last year. There are countless beautiful lakes where you can go kayaking, fishing, white water rafting, etc. You name it. I met some really cool world travelers at the campsite that evening. We spent our evening playing music and share stories under the stars.

　　我去年在賈斯柏國家公園裡玩得很開心。那裡有數不清的湖泊，在那裡你可以划塑膠皮艇、釣魚，和泛舟等等。你說的出來的都有。我那天晚上在營地也遇到很多很酷的正在環遊世界的人。我們那天晚上就在星空下玩音樂和分享彼此的故事中度過。

I scored big when I was in Yosemite National Park. Camping is relatively affordable for accommodations already. However, the fee to camp at Yosemite ranged from 6 to 26 dollars per night. I managed to secure a week for only 6 dollars per night. That was an unforgettable experience camping at such a beautiful place with so little expense. I was very pleased.

我在優美聖地國家公園裡拿到超好的優惠。露營本來就在住宿裡算比較負擔得起的了。但是在優美聖地裡露營的費用從六塊美金到二十六塊美金一個晚上不等。我竟然預訂到了一個禮拜每天晚上六元美金的而已。用那麼少的花費在那麼美的地方露營真是一個難忘的經驗。我超滿意的。

03
Question

What is the best or worst thing about camping?
露營最棒或是最糟的是什麼？

Michelle
蜜雪兒

The worst thing is that I don't understand why people make such a big fuss about camping. If you want to sleep outdoors then just sleep at your yard. Otherwise, if I'm traveling, I want to enjoy my stay. Preferably at hotels.

最糟的是我不懂為什麼大家要對露營那麼小題大作。如果你想要睡在戶外的話，為什麼不要睡在你家庭院就好了。不然，如果是我在旅行的話，我想要享受我的旅程。最好是在飯店裡。

Matt
麥特

Best thing about camping is that I feel free instead of being confined in four-walled houses. I can get dirty and go to my bed. I can make a camp fire and play music with my friends or friends to be. Additionally, there's no better lullaby than the nature. I sleep like a baby when I'm camping.

露營最棒的是我覺得很自由，而不是被四面牆的房子限制住。我可

以玩得很髒然後就回我的床上睡覺。我可以建一個營火然後就和我的朋友，或是即將成為朋友的人們玩音樂。除此之外，沒有什麼是比大自然更棒的催眠曲。我每次露營都睡得超熟的。

Becca
貝卡

The best thing about camping is its low cost. When you are on the road, camping can really save you a lot of budget. If you plan it right, you can have a very comfortable stay and with almost no cost. Why would anyone want to pass on that?

露營最棒的事就是他的低消費。當你在旅行的時候，露營真的可以幫你省下很多預算。如果你計劃的好的話，你還可以幾乎不花錢的住得很舒服。我不懂怎麼會有人想要錯過這個？

 ## Useful expressions

▲ **quality time** 親密時光

❶ Even though she's a career mom, she always makes sure to spend quality time with her kids.

即時她是一個職業婦女，她總是確保她有和她的小孩度過親密時光。

⛵ **grow on** 感染，影響

❷ At first, I didn't understand her dressing style, but I think it's growing on me now.

一開始的時候我很不懂她的穿衣風格，但是現在我好像慢慢開始懂了。

⛵ **touch base with** 和…聯繫

❸ We need to touch base with mom. We've been gone for too long.

我們應該要跟媽媽聯絡。我們出門好久了。

⛵ **eat me alive** 生吞

❹ The mosquitoes always eat her alive if she doesn't have pants on.

如果她沒穿長褲的話，蚊子總是會將她生吞。

⛵ **have a blast** 玩得很開心

❺ She had a blast on her twenty first birthday.

她在她二十一歲生日玩得十分開心。

⛵ **make a big fuss** 小題大作

❻ She always makes a big fuss when it comes to traveling.

只要是跟旅行有關的她就會小題大作。

露營

8 Unit

Hiking
爬山健行

 背景起源

What is a better way to immerse yourself in nature than hiking? Walking among forests, trees, lakes, rivers, waterfalls, jungles... with only a bag of necessities on you, you don't feel more down to earth than this. Sweats are dripping down, legs are getting sore, but you feel more aware and focused at the present nevertheless. Hiking is also a very popular activity to do, and there are groups of people that would identify themselves as the "hikers". What is so fascinating about this activity is that it doesn't require too much for you to do it. Almost everyone can do it, and there are a variety of trails for everyone to enjoy. Perhaps it's time to step away from our electronic devices and get in touch with your friends and your true self in the simplest form.

有什麼是比健行更好的辦法來沈浸在大自然之中？走在森林、樹、湖、小河、瀑布、叢林…等等之中，而身上只帶了一個背包大小的必需品，沒有什麼比這樣還要腳踏實地了。你的汗在滴，腳也越來越痠，但是你卻越來越察覺到周遭以及專注在現在。健行是一個很受歡迎的活動，而且也有一些人自稱他們為「登山客」。這個活動這麼吸引人是因為它沒有太多的門檻。幾乎每個人都可以健行，而且也有很多種步道供大家選擇。也許是時候放下你的電子產品並且用最簡單的方式來和你的朋友和自己聯絡感情了。

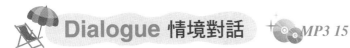

Dialogue 情境對話　MP3 15

June went to Africa to hike Mt. Kilimanjaro and she met a girl Sofia from Denmark on the trail.
瓊去了非洲健行吉力馬扎羅山，在步道上她認識了從丹麥來的蘇菲雅。

June: Are you hiking alone on this trail, too?	瓊：你也是自己來爬這個步道嗎？
Sofia: Yeah, I've always wanted to hike this trail, but no one wants to come with me, so...	蘇菲雅：對啊，我一直都很想來爬這個步道，沒有人要陪我來，所以我就來啦…
June: That's cool. Same here! No one thought I'd really go, so I want to prove them wrong.	瓊：酷喔！我也是！沒有人覺得我真的會來，所以我想要證明他們是錯的！

Sofia: There you go, girl! We can do this. It's going to be a great experience. I'm so excited.

蘇菲雅：那就對啦！我們可以的！這會是一個很棒的經驗。我好興奮喔！

June: Yeah, the only thing that worries me a little is the high altitude we're hiking into. I don't want to get the altitude sickness. That'll suck.

瓊：對啊，我唯一有點擔心的是我們會健行到高緯度的地方。我不想要得高山症！那樣就完蛋了！

Sofia: Well...at least we have a tour guide and the porters. Worst case they'll carry you down. You're so light. I'm sure they can do it!

蘇菲雅：嗯…至少我們有導遊還有挑夫。最慘的話他們也可以背你下去。你那麼輕，他們沒問題的！

June: That's comforting. Did you see how they carry the bags on their heads? They are so skilled!

瓊：我覺得安心多了。你有看到他們把包包背在頭上的樣子嘛？超厲害的！

Sofia: I know. They must have done this trail thousands of times though.

蘇菲雅：對啊！他們一定已經爬過這個步道上千次了！

June: Yeah, I think we'll hike around 7 hours today.

瓊：對啊。我想我們今天會爬大概七個小時。

Sofia: Yep, I asked the tour guide before we came and he told me today we'll hike for around 7 hours. They brought a chef, too, so we'll eat good tonight!

蘇菲雅：嗯對！我早先出發前有問導遊，他說今天我們大概會走七個小時。他們也有帶廚師，所以我們今天晚上應該會吃得不錯。

Sofa: I guess the only thing that surprises me is the amount of hikers here. It's so crowded. I was expecting some solo and exclusive hiking experience.

蘇菲雅：我想唯一讓我意外的是來這健行的人超多的！好多人喔！我還在想說這會是一個單獨的、獨家的健行體驗。

June: Haha...at least that's what the ads said, right?

瓊：哈哈…至少他們廣告是這麼打的啦，對不對？

01
Question

What kinds of hikes do you enjoy?
你喜歡怎麼樣的健行呢？

Michelle
蜜雪兒

What makes you assume that I like hiking? Some people love hiking and some people hate it. Personally, I don't really like any kind of hiking. I don't see the point of walking for miles and miles up and down mountains. You get all sweaty and out of breath. The worst thing is that the next day all your muscles ache. Of course it'll rain, and you'll get soaking wet. If it's sunny, you'll get sunburn. To make things really bad, you might fall over and twist your ankle or get stung by a bee.

　　你怎麼覺得我會喜歡健行呢？有的人喜歡健行，有的人不喜歡。我個人不怎麼喜歡健行啦。我不懂為什麼要長途跋涉的爬上山，再爬下來。你會流汗，然後喘不過氣。最糟的是隔天你全身的肌肉都會痠痛。當然你健行的時候會下雨，然後你就會變落湯雞。如果是晴天的話，你就會被曬傷。再更糟的是，你可能會跌倒然後扭到你的腳踝還是被蜜蜂螫到。

I don't mind hills, but I prefer a varied terrain or scenery to keep it fun. I also enjoy hikes that end with a waterfall. After you got all sweaty hiking, it'd be so nice to jump in the water to get reenergized.

我是不介意爬一些坡度，但是我比較喜歡有不一樣的地形和風景讓健行的時候比較好玩。我也很喜歡有一些步道的終點是瀑布。在你健行完流很多汗的時候，可以跳進水裡充電一定很棒！

I like to stop frequently to enjoy the scenery, the view, and the flora and the fauna, so it's best when the hike has a great view for me to stop and take pictures; preferably a

shaded hike, just so that it's more comfortable walking long distances.

我很喜歡一直停下來享受周遭的風景、景色、還有花草跟動物,所以如果是一個可以一直讓我停下來拍照的漂亮步道最好。更好的是還有遮蔭的步道,所以長途走下來也比較舒服。

What are some of the conversation topics you like to use during a long hike?
你在很長的健行旅程中都喜歡聊哪一些聊天的話題呢?

Michelle
蜜雪兒

I don't really do long hikes, but when I'm doing some repetitive workouts with my friends at the gym, we'd like to ask each other riddles. It's fun, and it really <u>takes your mind off</u> the boring task you're doing at the time. You don't believe me? How many months have 28 days?

我不作長途健行,不過如果我是跟我朋友在健身房裡做一些反覆的運動的話,我們喜歡互相問謎語。很好玩而且也可以幫你忘記你手邊的運動。你不相信我嗎？有幾個月份是有二十八天的？

Matt
麥特

My friends and I love to identify the plants and fungus along the way or share some crazy stories from our trips. A lot of the topics are really random, too. For example, where are some of the weirdest tattoos you have ever seen? On the way back though, we like to talk about how many pizzas we are going to slay when we get back.

　　我朋友和我喜歡辨識路上的植物或是菌類，我們也喜歡互相分享一些旅行的瘋狂事蹟或是聊一些超無厘頭的話題，像是你看過最奇怪的刺青是什麼？在回程的時候，我們喜歡聊回去之後要大吃幾個披薩。

Becca
貝卡

My friends and I are always contemplating our next purchase and swapping notes, <u>pros and cons</u>. It's really

good because I feel like we are utilizing time well, and we really got some good advice from each other. However, we also like to gossip about each other's relationships or our mutual friends'. Girls will always be girls.

我和我朋友最常一起討論我們下一個要買的東西，我們會交換意見然後做一些優劣分析。我覺得很好因為我們有好好地利用時間在對的事情上，而且我們也有得到很好的建議。不過啦，我們也喜歡八卦彼此的感情狀態，或是共同朋友的。啊呀，女生就是這樣嘛！

03 Question	What is the best hike you have ever done? How was it? 你健行過最好的步道是哪裡？那個步道怎麼樣呢？

Michelle
蜜雪兒

The best hike I have ever had or done is the Inca Hike in Peru. Don't get me wrong, I enjoy hiking, but it just needs to be fine-tuned. I joined this luxurious package where you get to get gourmet meals with champaign every night, and enjoy the only hot showers on the trail. What's better? I got massages every night when I was on the trail. I thought that was an excellent remedy for my aching muscles. That was a pretty good hiking experience.

我去過或唯一健行過最棒的步道是秘魯的印加古道。別誤會我喔，健行這個活動只要微調一下，我其實是喜歡健行的。我有參加這個豪華的行程，每天都可以吃美食加上香檳，然後享用步道上唯一的熱水澡。更棒的是什麼？我每天晚上都有按摩。那真是對我健行後痠痛的肌肉很好的治療。那個健行的經驗是還不錯啦。

Matt
麥特

The best hike I've ever done is the trek to Everest Base Camp in Nepal. The people are incredible. The scenery can't be beat, and you get to take a look at Mt. Everest or Chomolungma, which means the "Goddess Mother of the World." It's spectacular just to see the highest point on planet Earth. In May, the rhododendrons are in bloom with orchids growing in them. There are guesthouses on the way up. You can get a beer. Who knows, I might wander up there again.

我去過最棒的是尼泊爾的聖母峰基地營健行。那裡的人都好得不可思議，無敵的風景，而且你還可以看到聖母峰，或是 Chomolungma（聖母峰藏文），也就是世界之母的意思。可以從世界最高點看下去真的是很壯觀。在五月的時候，杜鵑花會和蘭花一起盛開。在上去的路上也會遇到民宿，而你也可以在那買瓶啤酒。誰知道，我可能會在遊蕩上去一次。

Becca
貝卡

No doubt the hike that circles Mont Blanc—the rooftop of Western Europe—is one of the best hiking experiences I have ever had. You travel through three different countries (France, Italy, Switzerland). But it's the civilization in between that really makes the trail special. Stop at villages or huts along the way to gorge yourself with fondue, wine, slices of local cheeses, and homemade bread—then keep walking to work it all off. It's all about motivations, isn't it?

毫無疑問那個環繞勃朗峰的步道，西歐的屋脊，是我最棒的健行經驗之一。你會經過三個不一樣的國家（法國、義大利和瑞士）。但是讓這個步道很特別的地方是在步道中的文明。你可以停留在小鎮或是路上的小茅屋去吃起司鍋、喝美酒、或是一片當地的起司，和手工作的麵包，然後再繼續往前走去把這些熱量都消耗掉。健行就是要有動力，不是嗎？

 Useful expressions

▲ **take your mind off…** 轉移你從…上的注意力；不要一直想…

❶ Watching a movie usually helps taking my mind off the work.

看電影通常都可以幫助我不要一直想著工作。

▲ **X will always be X** …永遠就是這樣

❷ They never grow up! Boys will always be boys.

他們永遠都不會長大！男生就永遠都是這樣。

▲ **work it off** 消耗掉…

❸ I gained so much weight from the past month. I have to work it off soon.

我過去這個月胖好多喔！我要趕快消耗掉這些多餘的體重！

9 Fishing
釣魚

 背景起源

Fishing is an ancient practice that can be dated back to 40, 000 years ago. Catching fish was necessary back then for the food source. However, in this era, not all people fished for food. There were also people who were just into the thrills of catching fish. It's the suspense of not knowing what you might catch, and the effort you put into while fighting the fish that get many people addicted. It feels like Christmas sometimes. You never know what presents you might get! The little taps you feel from the fishing poles and the patience it takes for the big fish to knock on your door are all part of the fun. Who says fishing is always relaxing? Back then, the fishermen would never understand why people caught fish and released them. Fortunately, more fishermen realize that in order to make fishing sustainable, we can't overfish! When you go fishing, don't forget to read about the local fishing regulations! Keep the fish in the ocean!

釣魚是一個可以追溯回四萬年前人們就會做的古老的事。在過去，人們抓魚是為了食物的來源，可是在現在這個時代，並不是所有的人釣魚都是為了要吃。也有很多人釣魚是為了抓到魚的刺激感。也就是那不知道會抓到什麼魚的懸疑，還有你跟魚大戰的時候讓很多人迷上釣魚。其實有時後釣魚就好像是聖誕節一樣，你永遠都不知道你會拿到什麼禮物！釣魚桿上你感覺到的輕敲，還有要等候大魚來敲門的耐心也都是釣魚好玩的一部分。誰說釣魚一定是很輕鬆的？在以前的時候，漁夫一定不會瞭解怎麼現在會有人抓到魚又釋放掉魚。慶幸的是，越來越多漁夫瞭解到為了讓釣魚永續發展，我們不能捕撈過度。當你去釣魚的時候，一定要記得先看當地的釣魚規則是什麼喔！我們要讓魚繼續活在海裡！

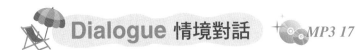

Dialogue 情境對話 *MP3 17*

Pete went on a charter boat in Japan for deep sea fishing. He is talking to the fishing guide Yusuke.

彼特去日本和其他人包船出海深海釣魚。他正在和釣魚的導遊裕介聊天。

Pete: Do you guys usually catch a lot of big fish here?

彼特：你們在這通常都會釣到大魚嗎？

Yusuke: Yeah, there are a lot of yellow fins they get pretty big here. You'll never know. It just might be your lucky day today!

裕介：對啊，這裡有很多黃耆尾魚，而且他們會長到蠻大的。誰知道，今天可能就是你釣到喔！

Pete: I am more than ready! Everyone has such professional setups. Hopefully, I will catch something among them.

彼特：我準備好了！大家都有好專業的設備喔。希望我可以在他們之中釣到一些什麼。

Yusuke: Fishing is not about setups. You got this Pete! I have faiths in you!

裕介：釣魚跟裝備沒什麼關係。你可以的彼特！我對你有信心！

Pete: Thanks man, I appreciate it. Oh wait, I think something is biting my bait.

彼特：謝啦！謝謝你對我的信心！等一下，好像有什麼東西在咬我的餌。

Yusuke: Really? Get ready to set the hook! Yank the pole hard the next time it bites.

裕介：真的嗎？準備好鉤住那條魚！下一次牠咬的時候用力拉漁竿。

Pete: I GOT IT!!!!

彼特：我抓到了！！！

Yusuke: Now, reel in the fish slowly, nice job Pete!

裕介：好現在慢慢把魚拉進來，做得好彼特！

Pete: It's a fighter whatever it is. It won't let me take any line.

彼特：不管彼是什麼它都很強壯。他不讓我拉進任何線。

Yusuke: Keep the line tight! We want to meet the fish.

裕介：把線拉緊！我們想要看到這條魚！

(15 minutes later)

（十五分鐘後）

Yusuke: It's a Mahi! Nice work!

裕介：是一條鬼頭刀！做得好！

Pete: Oh cool!! It must be around 40 pounds!!! I'm so exhausted! I totally didn't expect catching something like this!

彼特：喔好酷喔！牠應該有 40 磅（18 公斤）喔！我好累喔，我完全沒想到會釣到這個！

Yusuke: Nice catch! Put it in the cooler! Now we're fishing! We still have one full day! Let's catch some more fish Pete! That was exciting watching you fight the fish!

裕介：很不錯的魚耶！把牠放到冰箱裡！我們開始釣到魚囉！而且我們還有一整天！繼續釣多一點魚吧彼特！剛看你拉這條魚進來真刺激！

Pete: The fish is totally biting here. I'm coming back every year.

彼特：在這裡魚有在咬喔！我每年都要回來釣魚！

釣魚

01 Question

Are you interested in fishing? Why? Why not?

你對釣魚有興趣嗎？為什麼有或為什麼沒有？

Michelle
蜜雪兒

Not at all. I just don't like the smell of fish. Growing up, I would never like going to the fish market with my mother. I can't imagine catching them myself, let alone unhook them and all that work. Ew, and the baits. Oh my, I don't think it'll ever be my thing.

完全沒興趣。我就是不喜歡魚的味道。從小我就很不喜歡跟我媽媽去魚市。我無法想像自己抓魚，更別提把魚從鉤上拿下來還有所有那類的事。噁心，還有魚餌。我的天啊，我覺得我應該永遠都不會喜歡釣魚。

Matt
麥特

釣
魚

I'm very interested in fishing. It's so exciting when you have a fish on. I kept thinking whoever came up with fishing was such a genius. He must have been so thrilled when he found out it actually worked! It's actually a lot more complicated than what it looks like. How to tie the knots, hook on the baits, fight the fish, even how to reel the fish in. It just feels really good, when you do everything right and catch a fish yourself.

我對釣魚超有興趣的。魚上鉤的時候真的是超刺激的。我都一直在想當初第一個發明釣魚這件事的人真是一個天才。他那時候發現真的釣得到魚一定超興奮的！其實釣魚比看起來還要複雜很多。你要知道怎麼綁魚線的結，怎麼樣把魚餌勾在鉤上，怎麼鬥魚，怎麼把魚拉進來。當你把每一件事都做好然後再抓到魚的時候真的感覺超棒的！

Becca
貝卡

I'm somewhat interested I guess. I like to eat the fish to

say the least, but I have never been taught how to fish or I never had enough opportunities to fish. I'm interested in trying though. It just seems so relaxing and I guess for me it's not about catching, it's about being out there and enjoy being outdoors. I'm so tired of being trapped in the office.

我想我應該多少有一點興趣。至少我喜歡吃魚啦，但是從來沒有人教我釣魚或是我也沒什麼機會釣過魚。我蠻想要試試看的。好像蠻令人放鬆而且我想對我來說釣魚並不是真的要釣到魚，而是因為可以享受在戶外的時候。我真是受夠被關在辦公室了。

02
Question

What kind of fishing have you tried? How was it?
你試過怎麼樣的釣魚？好玩嗎？

Michelle
蜜雪兒

I tried fishing with my cousins at the lake in New Zealand. It was okay. None of us was really good at fishing, so we were just throwing the lines in the water, and hoping for the best. I was secretly hoping nothing would bite mine.

It was really more like flying a kite except that the lines were in the water. More like a social thing for us I would say.

我有在紐西蘭跟我的表姐妹試過。還好。我們其實都不太會釣魚，所以我們也只是把線丟到水裡，然後做最好的打算。其實我偷偷希望沒有東西會咬我的餌。那天其實真的比較像是在放風箏，只是我們是把線丟到水裡。 對我們來說，釣魚是比較像是在社交的活動。

Matt
麥特

I've tried a lot of different kinds of fishing. Deep-sea fishing, fresh water fishing, kayak fishing, Jet ski fishing, spear fishing...etc. You name it. I have to say that I like kayak fishing the best because kayaking is a good exercise and it's just you and your fishing poles out there. Really nice. I think everyone should try at least once.

我有試過很多不同種的釣魚。深海釣魚、淡水釣魚、皮艇釣魚、水上摩托車釣魚和魚叉獵魚等等。你說的出來的幾乎都有。不過我必須要說我最喜歡皮艇釣魚因為它是很好的運動，而且你只需要你和你的釣竿。真的很棒。我覺得每個人都要試試看這個。

釣魚

Becca
貝卡

I fished offshore one time at the beach with some friends. I mean, I wasn't really fishing. They set everything up for me to fish, and when we caught a fish, I reeled it in. It was really fun. We ended up grilling the fish on the beach. It was such a great night with friends and we ate the fish I caught!

我有跟朋友在海邊的岸邊釣魚過一次。其實我是說我朋友他們把一切都弄好，我沒有真的釣魚啦，只是我們釣到魚的時候，他們讓我拉起來。真的很好玩。而且我們後來就在海邊上烤魚。那真的是很棒的一晚，而且我們還吃了我抓到的魚！

03
Question

Why do you think people like fishing as a hobby?
你覺得為什麼會有人把釣魚當作一種興趣？

I know, right? Why do people like fishing as a hobby!... Oh wait, are you asking me? Hmm...I don't know. It's still a mystery to me. You beat me on this one. My best bet is that people are just running out of things to do. I don't have a clue on this one.

對啊，我知道。怎麼會有人把釣魚當作一種興趣！…喔你是在問我嗎？嗯…我不知道耶。對我來說還是一個謎。這題你真的考倒我了。我最好的猜測就是他們沒其他的事可以做了。我真的一點都不曉得。

Why would anyone not like fishing as a hobby is the real question to ask here. It's fun, and it can be both exciting and relaxing. You can possibly catch your own meals, and it's guaranteed fresh catch. Besides, it's extremely addicting. Once you try and you like it, it stays with you for a while.

怎麼會有人不把釣魚當作一種興趣才是真正要問的問題。它又好玩，既刺激又休閒。你有可能會抓到自己的食物而且還保證新鮮。除此之外，它真的是超級令人上癮。只要你試過一次，而且你也喜歡的話，你就會喜歡好長一陣子。

Becca
貝卡

I can see why people like fishing as a hobby. It's pretty mellow and you really don't need much to entertain yourself. Just a fishing pole with baits, a cooler and yourself. We're lucky that we can enjoy fishing differently than a lot of fishermen did back then. It must have been just catching and catching some more. I can see where the excitement comes when you catch one, too.

我可以懂為什麼大家喜歡把釣魚當作一種興趣。很放鬆而且你真的不需要太多東西來娛樂自己。只要有釣魚竿和餌，一個小冰箱和你自己。我們跟很多以前的漁夫比起來真的很幸運因為我們可以享受釣魚。我想以前大概就是釣魚，在釣多一點魚。我也可以理解為什麼釣魚很刺激。

Useful **expressions**

⚠ **knock on your door** …來敲門

❶ You have to work harder and don't let it go when happiness knocks on your door.

當幸福來敲門的時候，你要更努力不要讓它溜走。

⚠ **You never know. 很難說**

❷ You never know. Maybe she likes you, too!

很難說喔！搞不好她也喜歡你！

⚠ **It just might be your lucky day! 今天可能換你…**

❸ It just might be your lucky day to win a million dollars.

今天可能換你成為百萬富翁！

⚠ **You beat me on this one! 你考倒我了！**

❹ You beat me on this one! I really don't know the answer to it.

你考倒我了！我真的不知道這題的答案！

⚠ **I don't have a clue. 我不知道；我一點線索也沒有**

❺ I don't have a clue about where the school is.

我完全不知道學校在哪裡。

Unit 10

Yoga
瑜珈

背景起源

It is said that when yoga was first invented, it was designed as a warm up for the long-hour meditation to come. However, to many people, yoga is more than that. After twisting and turning your body and mind as much as you can, you learned to be more focused and flexible. It's an exercise not only for your body, but also for your mind and soul. Somewhere between inhaling and exhaling, the loads of the worries on your mind quietly unload and instead peace sneaks in your heart gently. Also, focusing in the present is something that is literally practiced within such exercise. While some say it is a very controlled exercise, others will tell you it's all about letting go. Whichever version of yoga you enjoy, let's give it a try. Namaste.

據說一開始發明瑜珈的時候，它是為了接下來長時間的靜坐所設計出的暖身運動。但是對很多人來說瑜伽不只是那樣而已。在你盡力地扭

116

轉你的身心之後，你會變得更專注和更柔軟。這個練習不止是針對身體而已，還有你的頭腦和心靈。大約在吸氣吐氣之間的某處，你心裡沈重的煩惱都默默地在那裡卸貨，而平靜則悄悄的湧上心頭。還有就是，專注在當下也是瑜伽確實在練習的一件事。當有的人跟你說瑜伽是一個十分克制的運動，其他人可能會跟你說瑜伽就是要放任你的身心。不管你比較喜歡哪個版本的瑜伽，試試看做瑜伽吧！我祝福你（瑜珈用語）。

Dialogue 情境對話　MP3 19

瑜珈

Brie and Libbie are volunteering at Costa Rica Yoga Farm for a month this summer.

布莉和利比今年暑假正在哥斯大黎加的 "Yoga Farm" 當志工。

Brie: I'm so glad I came here with you! How did you even find this place anyways? We're like in the middle of a jungle.

布莉：我超高興有跟你來的！你當初怎麼找到這個的？我們真的是在叢林裡面耶。

Libbie: Oh, you know how I am always very into yoga. I was just kind of browsing around on the Internet and just randomly saw this volunteering opportunity. I never like to be a tourist when I'm traveling, too. I'd rather stay at the place longer and

利比：喔，你知道我一直以來都很喜歡瑜珈。我只是隨便在網路上逛逛然後不小心就看到這個志工的機會。我旅行的時候從來就不喜歡當觀光客。我比較喜歡在

blend in with the locals. So I thought this was perfect.

一個地方待久一點，然後跟當地人混熟。所以我看到這個就想說太完美了！

Brie: Wow, seriously? So random! I know I wouldn't have chanced it if I were you, but I'm glad you did and thanks for inviting me to come along with you! Guided yoga classes, 3 healthy meals a day, and accommodation for a month only for $550. Are you kidding me? What a steal!

布莉：哇，真的假的？超隨機的！我知道如果我是你的話我一定不會決定要來，但是我超開心你決定要來而且還約我跟你來！瑜珈課，每天三個健康餐，加上一個月的住宿才五百五十美金。開什麼玩笑！超划算的！

Libbie: What do you think about the yoga classes here?

利比：你覺得這裡的瑜伽課怎麼樣？

Brie: I love that it is a yoga class, but everyone kind of jumps in and shares their knowledge about yoga here. And I love the open space here. It just makes so much sense to do yoga here...Like why wouldn't you do yoga here!?

布莉：我很喜歡雖然這是一堂瑜珈課，但是大家都會加入分享他們對瑜珈認知。而且我也很喜歡這裡開放的空間。在這裡做瑜珈超說得通的…在這裡有什麼道理不做瑜伽？！

Libbie: Haha...Yes I think you are on spot about the space here. I've been doing yoga two times a day here for half a month. That's something for me.

利比：哈哈⋯我覺得你對這裡的空間説的真的很對。我已經每天做瑜珈兩次半個月了。對我來説真的很厲害。

Brie: Yeah, although I feel pretty self-conscious around so many yogis here. Everyone does headstand like it's nothing, but oh well, we still have half a month to go!

布莉：對啊，不過我在這麼多做瑜伽的人面前做瑜珈我都覺得很害羞。大家在做倒立好像在走廚房一樣。但好啦，我們在這還有半個月！

Libbie: That's the spirit!

利比：這個精神就對了啦！

瑜珈

01 Question

What is your best yoga experience?
你最棒的瑜伽體驗是什麼？

Michelle
蜜雪兒

The best one is definitely the one that I went to a secluded private island in the Turks and Caicos with my parents. We stayed at the Parrot Cay Retreat. We had our daily yoga classes on a private beach, and it was followed by the most amazing SPA. They also have a yoga studio, which is 1,300 square feet if you wish to practice indoors. We also went to their outdoor Jacuzzi garden after the SPA. Hands down to the foremost relaxing yoga experience I've ever had.

最棒的一定是跟我爸媽去位在特克斯和凱科斯群島的一個私人島嶼。我們住在 Parrot Cay 渡假飯店。我們每天都會在一個私人海灘上上瑜珈課，然後再做超棒的 SPA。如果你想要在室內上瑜珈課的話，他們也有一千三百平方英尺大的瑜伽教室。我們做完 SPA 之後也會去他們室外的花園按摩池。這一定是我去過最令人放鬆的瑜伽體驗。

Matt
麥特

I think the time when I went to the Wanderlust Festival in Melbourne was a pretty memorable one. It was a huge event and there were so many people doing yoga and meditation with you. Everyone that joined the event was all really cool and with really positive vibes. It was definitely something different. I really had a great time.

我想我在墨爾本的時候參加的 Wanderlust 節還蠻令人印象深刻的。那是一個超大的活動，而且也有很多人在那跟你一起做瑜珈和靜坐。參加的人都很酷，而且也有很多正面的能量。真的是蠻不一樣的經驗。我真的玩得很開心。

Becca
貝卡

The first thing that <u>popped up in my mind</u> was the time

when I was traveling in Hawaii. I saw some groups of people doing yoga in the park. I approached them and understood that the practice was open to anyone and was donation-based. I thought that was such a cool thing, so I joined them the next day and from what I understood, 5 dollars was more than appropriate. Compared to regular classes for 15 dollars per class, that was so much better and I loved that we were doing yoga out in the open.

我第一個想到的就是在夏威夷的時候，我看到有一群人在公園做瑜伽。我跟他們接觸之後知道那是大家都可以參加的，而且下課之後是看你要捐贈多少錢的。我覺得很酷，所以我隔天就加入他們。據我所知，給五塊美金就蠻好的。跟一般十五塊的瑜伽課相比，真的好多了而且我也很喜歡我們是在戶外做瑜伽。

02 Question

What is your most embarrassing yoga moment?
你做瑜珈最尷尬的時候是？

Michelle
蜜雪兒

Oh, I personally don't remember one, but I can tell you a story from a friend of mine. So she said she was wearing these really cool and brand-named workout leggings. She's a pretty girl, so she didn't think it was so strange when she caught some people staring at her in class. However, it was not until a girl that was late for the class came to the spot in front of her did she realize that the girl was wearing the same pair of leggings as her. Those who see through when they were stretched out. You can only imagine how embarrassed I was...I meant she was...

喔，我個人我是不記得啦，不過我可以跟你說我一個朋友的故事。她說有一次她穿了一件很酷又是名牌的緊身運動褲。她很漂亮，所以當她看到班上有人盯著她看的時候她並不覺得很奇怪。但是，一直到有另外一個女生上課遲到，接著那個女生選了在她前面的位置，她發現那女生跟她穿的是同一條緊身褲。然後她才發現那些緊身褲撐開之後就會變成半透明的。你可以想像我那時候有多尷尬嗎…我是說她有多尷尬啦…

Matt
麥特

Haha the most embarrassing moment was definitely when I went to the yoga class right after dinner. A lot of yoga poses included twisting your body, and my stomach didn't like that too much. I started to feel like I needed to fart, but I tried to keep it down, but when we were doing the downward facing dog...I just couldn't help anymore...

哈哈，最尷尬的一定是我吃完晚餐就立刻去上瑜珈課的那次。那天很多姿勢都是要扭轉身體，我的胃不太喜歡那樣。我就開始覺得我想要放屁，但是我一直忍著。但是到我們要做下犬式的時候…我就再也忍不了…

Becca
貝卡

I normally go to the yoga class after work. That said, I'm usually pretty tired to begin with already. After a series of yoga flow, it always comes to the last pose, Savasana, or corps pose. I always fall asleep during the last pose. The most embarrassing moment was when I woke up one time, the other class was getting ready to start their session.

我通常工作後會去上瑜珈課。也就是說，我通常已經相當疲憊了，才要開始。在一系列的瑜珈律動後，總是到了最後的姿勢 Savasana 或者是 corps 姿勢。到最後姿勢期間我總是睡著了。最令人感到尷尬的時刻是，當我有次醒來時，其它的課程正準備開始他們下個課程。

Question 03
What is the most difficult part about yoga?
你覺得瑜珈最難的是什麼？

Michelle
蜜雪兒

This might sound rude, but I really can't understand my yoga instructor. I don't know if it's his accent or all those Sanskrit words. I am constantly lost in class. I just wish there's a translator in every class. Hey, you never know, that might be the next new thing!

聽起來可能很沒禮貌，但我真的聽不懂我的瑜伽老師在說什麼。我

不知道是他的口音還是那些梵文的問題。我在上課的時候都不知道他在說什麼。我真希望每堂課都有個翻譯。嘿,很難講喔,那可能會是下一個流行的事。

Matt
麥特

I consider myself as an active person, but when it comes to yoga, it's a totally different thing. I'm just not that flexible. I can't do a split just like that or locking my knees when I'm supposed to. Oh well, I'll get there some day.

我自己認為我是一個蠻好動的人,但是瑜珈完全是另外一回事。我柔軟度真的沒那麼好。我不會隨便就可以劈腿,或是當有需要的時候就把膝蓋伸直。唉,總有一天我會變那麼厲害的。

Becca
貝卡

Personally, I think the hardest part is that instead of very specific instructions, sometimes the teachers will use very abstract terms in class. Things like, "open your heart", or "focus on your third eye" ...etc. I just can't quite grasp the concept yet.

　我個人覺得最難的是瑜伽老師有時候都會用一些很抽象的話而不是很仔細的教法。例如：「敞開你的心胸」，還是「專注在你的第三眼」…等等。我真的還不太懂那些概念。

 ## Useful **expressions**

⚠ **namaste** 我祝福你，謝謝（瑜珈用語）

❶ Thank you for joining our yoga class today. Namaste.
謝謝你今天參與我們的瑜伽課。我祝福你。

⚠ **blend in** 混熟

❷ He always blends in a new environment very quickly.
他總是可以很快就跟新的環境混熟。

⚠ **What a steal!** 超划算的！超便宜的！

❸ I got the same dress on ebay with only half of the original price. What a steal!
我在 ebay 上用原價一半的價錢買到了一樣的洋裝。超划算的！

11 Sports
運動

Unit

 背景起源

Sports are very popular worldwide. However, different country enjoys different sports. Can you imagine while you grow up playing basketball, other kids on the other side of the world grow up surfing or skiing? It may sound bizarre when you meet people that have never heard of your favorite sport before, but likewise, they cannot believe you don't know their sports, either. It usually results from the natural settings of the country. Nevertheless, it is fun to keep the varieties in the world. When you go traveling, sports games are something that you can either enjoy watching or playing. Who says smile is the only <u>universal language</u>? Sports can serve the same purpose as well. You just might meet your best friend playing a sport together somewhere far away from home.

全世界都很喜歡運動。但是不一樣的國家喜歡不一樣的運動。你可以想像當你從小打籃球長大的時候，在世界的另一邊，其他小孩是衝浪長大或是滑雪長大的嗎？你可能會覺得很奇怪當你遇到有人沒聽過你最喜歡的運動是什麼，可是一樣的，他們可能也不敢相信你不知道怎麼玩他們的運動。這有可能是因為地域自然場景的不同。但是讓世界各地有不一樣的運動也很好玩啊。當你旅行的時候就可以看不一樣的運動比賽或是玩不一樣的運動。誰說只有微笑是世界共通的語言？我覺得運動也是一樣的。你可能會在離家很遠的地方遇到你最好的朋友！

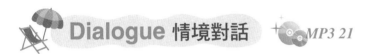 **Dialogue 情境對話** MP3 21

Erica is taking her friend Hilda who is visiting from Norway to a college football game.
艾瑞卡要帶她從挪威來的朋友希達去一個大學的美式足球賽。

Erica: Let's leave the house soon Hilda! Are you almost ready?

艾瑞卡：希達，我們要出門囉！你快準備好了嗎？

Hilda: What? When does the football game start again? I am <u>under the impression</u> that the game doesn't start until this evening!

希達：什麼？你說美式足球賽什麼時候開始啊？我一直以為是今天晚上才要開始！

Erica: You're right, but we have to be there at 1pm for the tailgating!

艾瑞卡：對啊，但是我們一點就要過去停車場野餐會。

Hilda: What is tailgating?

希達：停車場野餐會是什麼？

Erica: Oh my gosh, you're going to love it. It's really fun. Everyone will drive their car there to secure a spot at the parking lot, and then they'll open their trunks and just barbeque there. There will be great foods, music and drinks!

艾瑞卡：我的天啊，你一定會很愛的。真的很好玩。大家都會把他們的車開到停車場佔個好位置，然後他們就會打開後車廂，然後就在那烤肉。有好吃的食物，音樂還有喝的！

Hilda: Oh wow, it sounds like a great time! But won't you be exhausted by the time the game starts?

希達：喔哇！聽起來好好玩喔！但是等到比賽真的開始的時候大家不會就累壞了嗎？

Erica: No way, tailgating helps warming up the game! That's when you know you're going to have a great game when you tailgate.

艾瑞卡：才不會呢，停車場野餐會是幫比賽暖場！當你們有先去停車場野餐會的時候，你就知道那天的比賽會超好玩的！

Hilda: Sounds good! What should we bring? I'm clueless. This is going

希達：聽起來好棒！那我們要帶什麼？我完全

to be my first tailgating experience.

沒頭緒。這是我第一個停車場野餐會。

Erica: <u>I got you covered.</u> I've already marinated some meat and we're going to meet my friends down there. They have the grills and everything set up. We just have to show up!

艾瑞卡：有我在，別擔心。我已經醃了一些肉，然後我們會去跟我的一些朋友會合。他們已經把烤肉架還有其他東西架好了，我們只要出現就好了！

Hilda: Excellent!

希達：太棒了！

 三問三答 ＋ MP3 22

01 Question Have you been to any sports game? How was it?
你有去看過任何運動的比賽嗎？好玩嗎？

 Michelle 蜜雪兒

I was invited to the 2015 FIFA Women's World Cup in

Canada because a friend I grew up with was playing for USA. I got the VIP seats to watch the game and joined them for the after party to celebrate the victory. It was quite an experience to witness my friend add World Cup Champion to her already amazing career.

我有一個從小長大的朋友他代表美國隊參賽，所以我受邀去加拿大看 2015 年的女子世界盃足球賽。我有 VIP 座位，而且後來還加入她們慶祝勝利的派對。親眼看到我朋友把世足冠軍列入她本來就很好的職業生涯真的是很棒的經驗。

Matt
麥特

I went on a road trip in California. It was during the time of the NBA playoffs, we couldn't pass the game in Los Angeles when the Lakers are playing against the Miami Heats. It was quite an exciting game to watch. You can't beat live NBA playoffs. It was totally worth the drive.

我到加州公路旅行，那個時候正好是 NBA 季後賽的時候，所以我們不想錯過在加州的湖人隊跟邁阿密熱火隊的賽事。那場比賽真的很刺激，而且你真的無法超越現場的 NBA 季後賽。完全值得我們開那麼遠的車去看。

Becca
貝卡

I watched a college volleyball game in Italy when I was doing the exchange student program. I didn't know what to expect, but they were actually really skilled. Apparently, it has become a very popular sport in Italy. It was really fun watching the game for sure.

運動

我在義大利當交換學生的時候去看了一場大學排球賽。我不知道該預期什麼，但是他們真的很厲害耶。很顯然的在義大利，排球已經漸漸成為一個蠻受歡迎的運動。至少是很好看的比賽。

02
Question

Which was one special sport you tried on your trip? Did you like it?
你有在旅行的時候嘗試過什麼特別的運動嗎？你喜歡嗎？

I tried the Aerial Yoga in New York City when I was on a business trip last time. It definitely turned my world upside down. It's basically the combination of Yoga and Pilates with the use of a hammock. I felt really good after the workout.

我上次去紐約市出差的時候有試過空中瑜珈。那真的是把我的世界弄得翻天覆地的。那其實就是用吊床來練習瑜珈和皮拉提斯的綜合版。我在運動後真的覺得很棒。

I tried wake surfing in Moscow. It's really cool because you are basically surfing the wake created by the boat in front of you. Who knows that you can surf in a lake as well? I mean it's nothing crazy, but it's awesome to get on your board and have some fun.

我在莫斯科有嘗試尾流衝浪。那很酷因為你就是在衝你前面的船幫你製造出來的浪。誰知道你也可以在湖上衝浪？我是說，那沒有衝很瘋狂的浪還是什麼的，可是可以拿你的板子出來就玩得很開心真的很棒。

Becca
貝卡

I tried Capoeira when I was in Brazil. It was really spontaneous because I was walking down the street from my hostel when I ran into a group of people circled together doing this thing called Capoeira. It was somewhere between martial art and awkward dancing. One of them actually asked me to try it with them, and I did! He might have regretted inviting me to do it because I had no idea what I was doing, but I'm glad I tried!

我去巴西的時候有試過卡波耶拉。那真的很隨性因為我只是從我的青年旅社走出來，然後就遇到一群人圍成一個圈圈在做這個叫做卡波耶拉的運動。那其實有點是在武術和很拙劣的舞蹈中間。他們其中一個人叫我加入他們一起嘗試看看，然後我就試試看了。他可能有後悔邀請我一起因為我真的不知道我在幹嘛，但是我還是很高興我試了一下。

運動

03
Question

What sport do you want to learn? Why?
你有特別想要學什麼運動嗎？為什麼？

Michelle
蜜雪兒

I've always wanted to try horseback riding. What's not to love about horses? I loved riding the ponies ever since I was a child, but there's a fine line between reality and fantasy. There were several times when I finally decided to do it, I chickened out the second I went on the horseback. Oh well...

　　我一直以來都很想學騎馬。馬有什麼值得你討厭的？我從小就很喜歡騎小馬，但是現實跟幻想之間就是有點不同。有好幾次我終於決定要去學，可是一騎上馬背我就退縮了。就是這樣囉…

I want to <u>get into</u> rock climbing. I think it's such a great exercise and it'll be a good skill to have when I'm traveling. You never know. I also heard that helps you to become stronger as a person as well. There are a lot of fear factors when you are dangling from high above, and you just have to take <u>the leap of faith</u> to get to the next step!

我想要學攀岩。我想那會是一個很好的經驗，而且在旅行的時候那也會是一個很好的技能。一切都很難說。而且我聽說攀岩也可以幫助你成為一個更堅強的人。當你懸逛在高處的時候，有很多令你害怕的事情，可是你就是要有信心地跳躍過去下一步。

運動

I think Zumba will be a good sport to learn! I tried it once in Panama, and I really had so much fun even if I had no idea what I was doing. It's pretty much a dancing sport. I think it'll be something I'll stay interested for a while. And

did I mention the music rocks?

　　我覺得尊巴會是一個很好的運動！我有在巴拿馬試過一次。就算我當時一點都不知道我在幹嘛，可是我還是玩得好開心。那其實就是一個跳舞的運動。我想那是一個我會喜歡蠻久的運動。而且我有說尊巴的音樂超棒的嗎？

 Useful expressions

🔺 **universal language** 世界共通的語言

❶ Many people want to learn English because they think English is the universal language.

很多人想要學英文是因為他們覺得英文是世界共通的語言。

🔺 **under the impression** 以為，覺得

❷ I'm still under the impression that she might be interested in going out with me.

我還是覺得她想要跟我約會。

🔺 **I got you covered.** 有我在！

❸ Don't worry about the classes. I will tell the teachers that you are very sick now and I will take notes for you. I got you covered.

你不用擔心上課。我會跟老師講你病得很嚴重，我也會幫你做筆記。有我在別擔心。

⛵ **turn my world upside down** 讓我的世界神魂顛倒；讓我的世界翻天覆地的。

❹ She turned my world upside down ever since I met her. I don't know what to do.

自從我認識她之後，她就讓我的世界神魂顛倒。我不知道該怎麼辦。

⛵ **there's a fine line between** 在…之間還是有一線之隔

❺ There's still a fine line between flirty and creepy. You should not follow her home.

在調情還有鬼祟之間還是有一線之隔。你不應該要跟蹤她回家的。

⛵ **chicken out** 退縮

❻ He chickened out the second he was going to tell her his feelings.

他在要跟她說他對她的感覺時就退縮了。

⛵ **get into** 進入…的領域

❼ She wants get into fashion design, but she doesn't have any connection.

她想要進入時尚設計圈，可是她沒有任何人脈。

⛵ **the leap of faith** 信心的跳躍，義無反顧的行動

❽ Sometimes you just have to take the risk and the leap of faith.

人生有的時候你就是應該要冒點險，義無反顧的行動！

12 Water Sports
水上活動

Unit

 背景起源

Did you know that there is about 71 percent of the earth's surface is water and only 29 percent is land-covered? With around 7.3 billion people living on earth, we started to expand our playground towards the water. There are all sorts of activities we can do in the water, and with some practice, many more people are introduced to such sports. Almost all of us have wonderful memories playing in the water. Be it swimming, snorkeling, or sailing, people are always drawn to the ocean. However, when you are in the water, make sure you know your limit and risks before you enter the water.

你知道地球表面有百分之七十一都是水嗎？只有百分之二十九是陸地。而陸地上有大約七十三億人口，所以我們就開始朝著水源開闊我們可以玩耍的地方。在水裡我們可以做很多不一樣的活動，而在多家練習之後，越來越多人開始了水上活動。我們幾乎在水上玩耍都有很好的回憶，不管是游泳、浮潛，還是風帆，大家總是被水吸引。但是當你在水裡的時候，要知道自己的極限在那裡，還有在下水前知道潛在的風險是什麼。

 ## Dialogue 情境對話 MP3 23

Nina and Lavery are hiking to the Kealakekua Bay, Big Island, for snorkeling.
妮娜和拉佛立正在要去夏威夷大島的凱阿拉凱庫灣浮潛。

Nina: This isn't a bad hike at all. I don't get why people are so intimidated about hiking down this trail.	妮娜：這個步道一點都不會不好啊。我不懂為什麼大家那麼怕來爬這個步道。
Lavery: Well, we are going downhill now, so naturally it's easy. Wait till we have to climb back up the hills.	拉佛立：嗯，因為我們現在在走下坡啊，所以當然很簡單。等我們爬上坡的時候你就知道了。
Nina: If you're trying to scare me, it's working. It is pretty steep, too. I can't imagine having to climb back up. How far is this trail anyways?	妮娜：如果你是想要嚇我的話，很有用喔！而且這裡蠻陡的。我無法想像要爬回來。這個步道到底多長啊？

Lavery: I'm not exactly sure, but there are 8 markers, and each is around ¼ mile or more.

拉佛立：我也不太確定，但是這裡總共有八個標示牌。每一個都大概四分之一英里（四百公尺）。

Nina: What?! And all this time, we've only passed 1 marker?

妮娜：什麼！？我們到目前為止只有經過一個標示牌？

Lavery: Yep, not trying to scare you, but I just want to prepare you.

拉佛立：對啊，我沒有要嚇你啦，我只是想要讓你有心理準備。

(1 hour and half later)

（一個半小時後）

Nina: The snorkeling is better to be good here!! I'm soooo ready to jump in the water.

妮娜：這裡的浮潛最好很棒！我已經超級無敵準備好要跳到水裡了。

Lavery: Let's do it. The visibility of the water seems amazing today!

拉佛立：我們走吧！今天水裡的能見度超棒的！

Nina: Oh wait a minute, are those sharks?? Look at those fins!!

妮娜：等等，那些是鯊魚嗎？你看那些鰭！

Lavery: No, that's an eagle ray! Today is our lucky day! They look just like angles when they are swimming!

拉佛立：不是啦，那些是燕魟！我們今天真幸運！他們在游泳的時候看起來會很像天使！

Nina: Are those dangerous?

妮娜：他們會危險嗎？

Lavery: No, not at all. They are not aggressive! Cross my heart.

拉佛立：不會啦，一點都不會。他們沒有攻擊性！我保證。

Nina: Okay, let me get my fins and snorkels ready.

妮娜：好，讓我穿一下我的蛙鞋和浮潛裝備。

Lavery: Dolphins!! I'm going in first Nina! I'll see you on the flipside!

拉佛立：海豚！我要先跳下去了喔妮娜！待會見！

Nina: Wait up!

妮娜：等我一下啦！

水上活動

 三問三答 MP3 24

01
Question

What is your favorite water sport? Why?
你最喜歡的水上活動是什麼？為什麼呢？

Michelle
蜜雪兒

I don't like water sports...If I really have to pick one, I would probably go with snorkeling. It's pretty cool to peek in what's under the ocean without getting too involved. There are a lot of hotels that have snorkeling packages you can join or some hotels even have a pool you can swim with fish. If you want, of course.

　　我不喜歡水上活動…不過如果真的硬要選，我應該會選浮潛吧！可以看看海裡面有什麼是還蠻酷的，而且也沒有跟他們太近。很多飯店都會有浮潛的行程可以加入。有的飯店還會有游泳池是你可以在裡面浮潛，跟魚一起游泳的。當然是你想要的話啦！

Matt
麥特

My favorite water sport is definitely surfing. Nothing else can make you feel so free. And I'm more focus at the moment when I'm surfing. You have to observe your surroundings constantly and live in that moment because once you daydream, the wave is gone already. I learned a lot about life from surfing. Like how you should always be humble facing the ocean and I like to think of ocean as life in this case.

　我最喜歡的水上活動一定是衝浪。沒有任何事可以讓你覺得那麼自由自在。而且我在衝浪的時候會更專注在當下。你要一直觀察你周遭的環境，然後活在當下因為你只要一發呆，浪就過了。我從衝浪學了很多關於人生的道理。例如你面對海洋的時候一定要保持謙卑，而在這個例子裡，我也喜歡把海洋想成人生。

Becca
貝卡

My favorite water sport is diving. I love going diving

水上活動

when I'm troubled with_life. Every single noise just instantly goes away once I'm in the water. I can only hear my breath and the bubbles I created from the oxygen tank. It's a really relaxing and peaceful feeling down there.

我最喜歡的水上活動是潛水。每次我人生遇到難題的時候我就會去潛水。一下水，每個雜音都立刻消失。我只聽得到我呼吸的聲音和從氧氣筒呼吸時製造的泡泡聲。在水裡真的是很放鬆又很平靜的感覺。

02
Question

Do you know a secret spot for any water sport?
你知道任何水上活動的秘密地點嗎？

Michelle
蜜雪兒

I don't think it's a secret, but the Great Barrier Reef in Australia is always something people talk about when it comes to snorkeling or other water sports. Remember the campaign for the best job in the world back in 2009? The job was to take care of the Great Barrier Reef. I don't want to admit it, but I applied for the job as well...

我覺得這個應該不是秘密了，不過每次提到浮潛還是其他水上活動，大家就會提到澳洲的大堡礁。還記得 2009 年那個全世界最棒的工作的宣傳嗎？那個工作就是可以照顧大堡礁。我不想承認，可是我那時候也有應徵那個工作啦⋯

Matt
麥特

Have you heard about "Cloud 9"? It's a really good surf spot in the Philippines. They have some world-class waves there. It's not as crowded as many famous surf spots, and there are a lot of bed and breakfast there where you can stay for a cheap price with healthy meals there. I really enjoy my stay there every time I go.

你有聽過 "Cloud 9" 嗎？那是在菲律賓很有名的衝浪點。那裡不像很多其他有名的浪點一樣擁擠，在那裡你付很少錢就可以住在那裡的民宿，而且那裡還有提供健康的餐點。我每次去都玩得很開心。

水上活動

Becca
貝卡

There are a lot of turtle cleaning stations in the Hawaiian Islands. The turtle cleaning stations are just a huge flat rocks where turtles just come and sit on the rock and the little fish will come and clean their shells. It's really cool to watch them come in and get cleaned.

在夏威夷群島裡有很多的烏龜清洗站。烏龜清洗站其實就是一塊平坦的大石頭，烏龜們會來坐在那石頭上，然後很多小魚就會來清洗龜殼上的髒東西。看到烏龜們游來清洗他們的殼的時候真的很神奇。

03 Question

What is the scariest experience you had with water sports?
你有過最恐怖的水上活動的經驗是什麼？

Michelle
蜜雪兒

Scariest one was when I stood up paddling with some of

my girlfriends in Panama right in front of our resort. We were just enjoying ourselves out there when one of my friends screamed out "sharks!!" and pointed to the fins on the surface of the water. We all screamed together and tried to paddle away from it. We ended up paddling to a school of dolphins. It was truly a blessing in disguise.

最恐怖的就是我跟一些女生朋友在巴拿馬渡假飯店前站立式划槳的時候。當我們正玩得開心時,其中一個朋友突然尖叫:鯊魚!然後指著水裡的鰭。我們一起尖叫,然後儘快划離開那些鰭。結果我們到最後划著遇到一群海豚。那真的是因禍得福。

Matt
麥特

One time my buddy and I went kayaking, and the wind started to take us away from the shore very fast. We were drifting very fast from the shore. It was till the point when it was getting dark that we thought there was no way for us to paddle back. We called the Coast Guard for rescue. They sent in a helicopter to locate us and then a boat came and towed us back. It was a very close call.

水上活動

　　有一次我跟我的好朋友在划皮艇，結果風突然很快的把我們吹離岸邊。我們很快的漂離了很遠。直到天黑了我們才認知到我們已經划不回岸邊了。我們得打給海岸警備隊求救。他們叫了一架直升機來幫我們定位，然後一艘船再來把我們拖回去。當下真的很危急。

Becca
貝卡

　　When I was in Costa Rica. I signed up for a surfing lesson by the beach there. I had a lot of butterflies in my stomach before I went. Everything went very well, and it was such a fun experience until a set of big waves came in and washed me down in the water. The current was so strong that I was just tumbling in the waves. It felt like I was in a washing machine. Luckily, my surf instructor came and got me out of the water very fast.

　　我在哥斯大黎加的時候有在那裡的海邊報名衝浪課程。我在去之前很緊張，但是去了之後一切都很順利，而且也很好玩，直到突然有一陣陣的大浪來了，然後把我衝到水裡。水裡的急流很強，所以我就一直在浪裡翻滾。我那時候覺得我好像在洗衣機裡面一樣。好險我的衝浪教練及時把我從水裡很快的拉出來。

Useful **expressions**

⚓ **cross my heart 我保證**

❶ I will try my best to help you. Cross my heart!

我會盡全力幫你。我保證！

⚓ **see you on the flip side. 待會見，改天見**

❷ Thanks for hanging out today! I'll see you on the flip side.

謝謝你今天一起跟我玩阿！改天見！

⚓ **live in the moment 活在當下**

❸ You shouldn't worry too much about future. Just live in the moment!

你不應該太擔心未來，要活在當下！

⚓ **blessing in disguise 因禍得福**

❹ If I hadn't had that car accident, I wouldn't have met your mom. It was truly a blessing in disguise.

如果那個車禍沒發生的話，我就不會認識你媽。真是因禍得福。

⚓ **It was a close call! 真是危急，真的好險。**

❺ I almost fell off the car. It was a close call.

我差點就掉出車外了。真的好險喔！

水上活動

13
Unit

Music
音樂

背景起源

Music is one of those magical things that can bring you to an entirely different space instantly. Sounds bizarre and wild, but we all have the experience when you put on your earphones and certain songs take you down memory lane. The reason is because music is such a unique creation and no two songs are exactly the same (also with the great help of copyright). When you are traveling, you come across different types of music, and different melodies. It is the music that connects you and the memories you have when you travel. The lyrics, the rhythm, and the tone of a song say a lot about the place. In a way, it is a great way to travel around the world within an hour. Start collecting the music you encounter on the road, just in case you want to go back from time to time.

音樂是那些可以瞬間帶你到別的空間的神奇事物之一，聽起來很詭異又很狂野，可是我們都有在戴上耳機之後，某首歌曲帶我們回到某個回憶的經驗。原因是因為音樂是一個很獨特的創作，而且世界上沒有兩首歌是完全一模一樣的（加上還有智慧財產權的幫忙）。你在旅行的時候可能會遇到不一樣種類的音樂，和不一樣的旋律。就是那些音樂連結了你和你旅行的時候的回憶。歌詞、節奏，還有曲調都跟我們說了很多關於這個地方的事情。在某方面來說，這是一個在一個小時內環遊世界很好的辦法。開始搜集你旅行的時候遇到的音樂吧，以免有的時候你想要再回到那個地方。

 **Dialogue 情境對話** *MP3 25*

Jessica and Sam are going to the Open Mic night at a bar in San Francisco.
傑西卡和山姆正要去舊金山的一間酒吧參加 Open Mic（開放式麥克風）。

Jessica: Are you going to perform tonight?	傑西卡：你今天晚上要表演嗎？
Sam: I don't know. I guess we'll see what the vibe is like tonight.	山姆：我不知道耶。我想我們先看看今天晚上的氣氛怎麼樣好了。
Jessica: Oh, it's going to be great, and I'll be your biggest fan and make	傑西卡：喔，會很棒的啦，而且我會當你最大

a lot of noises.

的粉絲，然後製造很多噪音。

Sam: Haha...thanks Jessica, but that sounds horrible.

山姆：哈哈…謝啦傑西卡，但是聽起來很恐怖。

Jessica: Come on, Sam, you're such a great musician. You and your guitar are going to go far. Someone has to discover you.

傑西卡：拜託，山姆，你是那麼厲害的樂手耶。你和你的吉他一定會有很長的路可以走的。你應該要被挖掘的。

Sam: Thanks Jessica. You know what, I'll go if you go.

山姆：謝啦傑西卡。你知道怎樣嘛，如果你上台的話，我就上台。

Jessica: What, no way, I can't Acapella it.

傑西卡：什麼，才不要。我不會清唱啦。

Sam: I'll play guitar for you. Let's just do what we normally do. That sounds really good.

山姆：我會幫你彈吉他。我們就像平常那樣表演就好啦。那樣聽起來很棒。

Jessica: We were just <u>fooling around</u> though. Nobody wants to see me on stage.

傑西卡：我們只是在胡鬧而已耶。沒有人想看我上台啦。

Sam: I DO! It will be fun Jessica. You can play the drums, too. Let's <u>jam</u>!

山姆：我想啊！一定會很好玩的傑西卡。你也可以打鼓啊！我們來演奏啦！

Jessica: Alright, that sounds fun. Just like the vocal in Echosmith, huh? She always sings and plays drums.

傑西卡：好啦，聽起來蠻好玩的。就像史密斯迴聲樂團裡面的主唱一樣。她每次都一邊唱一邊打鼓。

Sam: There you go! I'm gonna go tell the manager here that we're performing.

山姆：那就對啦！我去跟這裡的經理說一下我們要上台。

Jessica: Oh my god Sam. We're leaving San Francisco tomorrow anyways.

傑西卡：我的天啊山姆。反正我們明天就要離開舊金山了。

Sam: You only live once! Let's do it.

山姆：你只活一回。我們上台吧。

音樂

Jessica: Maybe we'll have some fans that don't want us to leave.

傑西卡：搞不好我們還會有一些粉絲不想要我們離開。

Sam: hahaha...I'm ready for some fun!

山姆：哈哈哈…我已經準備好要好好玩一下了！

三問三答　MP3 26

01 Question

What is your favorite type of music?
你最喜歡的是哪一類的音樂呢？

Michelle
蜜雪兒

My favorite type of music is Jazz. It's the perfect music in the morning, in the afternoon and in the evening. I just can't get enough of it. There are so many emotions in Jazz and I always feel like when people are talking about music being contagious, I think they are referring to Jazz.

我最喜歡的音樂就是爵士樂。早上、下午和晚上聽都很棒。我就是聽不膩爵士啦。爵士樂裡有很多的情緒。當大家在說音樂很有感染力的時候，我都想說他們一定是在說爵士樂。

Matt
麥特

I'm gonna go with Reggae. I've been traveling in a lot of islands, and they start to grow on me one day, and before I know it, I'm humming the reggae tunes all day. It's a very relaxing, beach music really. I'm not too big of a dancer, either, but I can do the swing with Reggae music.

我應該是會選雷鬼樂。我已經在很多的島嶼旅行過了。突然有一天我漸漸開始喜歡雷鬼樂，然後在我反應過來之前，我已經整天都在哼雷鬼的調子了。那是一種很令人放鬆，海邊的那種音樂。我也不是很會跳舞，但是我可以跟著雷鬼樂搖擺。

音樂

Becca
貝卡

I think all my favorite songs belong to Indie Rock, so I assume that's my favorite type of music. You know how sometimes when you turn on the radio, and you just connect with the tunes, I think Indie Rock is my tune.

我覺得好像我很喜歡的歌都是獨立搖滾，所以我想那應該是我最喜歡的音樂種類吧！你知道有的時候你打開電台音樂，然後你就會蠻喜歡某一台的音樂，我想我喜歡的那台就是獨立搖滾。

02
Question

Where have you heard the best live music?
你在哪裡聽過最棒的現場的音樂？

Michelle
蜜雪兒

The best one was at the Preservation Hall in New Orleans. It's like the holy ground for all jazz fans. I had my doubts before it started because it was in a tiny and old building with no seats or air-conditioning, but when they started to perform, I had goose bumps, and I was listening in tears. Let's just put it that way.

　　我聽過最棒的是在紐奧良的典藏廳。那裡就像是爵士樂迷們的聖地一樣。我在表演開始之前有我的疑慮因為那棟建築又小又舊而且又沒有座位和冷氣。可是當他們開始演奏的時候，我全身起雞皮疙瘩，還含淚聽整個表演。這樣說你就懂了吧。

Matt
麥特

　　I was backpacking in New Zealand when my CouchSurfing host took me to this family fair. It was really fun with a lot of rides and food stands, but what caught my attention was this reggae band that was playing on stage. They are called Ketchafire and that was the best live music I've ever heard. It was just amazing really.

　　我在紐西蘭當背包客的時候，我沙發衝浪的主人帶我去一個家庭園遊會。那裡真的很好玩，而且也有很多遊樂設施和小吃攤，但是真正讓我注意到的是正在台上表演的雷鬼樂團。他們的名字是 Ketchafire 而

那也是我聽過最棒的現場的音樂。真的很棒！

I was walking at the underground of a park in Spain and that was when I came across this amazing street artist. He's a guitarist, and really all he did was just playing guitar, but the sound was very crisp with the echoes from the underground, it became very powerful music. There were people stopping <u>here and there</u>, but I stayed the whole time. I couldn't leave such a great performance. Of course, I gave him some money afterwards and bought the CD. The CD isn't quite the same as what I heard that day, but it's still great.

我在西班牙一個公園的地下道走路時，突然遇到這個超厲害的街頭藝人。他是一個吉他手，然後他真的也只是就是在彈吉他而已，但是吉他的聲音很清脆，而且因為在地下道有回音就讓整個音樂十分的強烈。我那時候停下來就走不開這個表演了。當然，我後來有給他一些錢還有買了他的 CD。CD 跟現場聽的時候不一樣，可是還是很棒。

03 Question

What's the most unique experience you have related to music?

你有關於音樂最獨特的經驗嗎？

Michelle
蜜雪兒

I was visiting some friends in Bogota, Colombia, and one night we went to this tiny bar where there was a singer singing some Latin love songs in the bar. Everything looked very normal until the singer walked to my friends, and asked them in Spanish what kind of music I like, I told him Reggaeton, which is like the Spanish version of Hip-Pop I really like back then. He walked back and talked to other musicians, and then he started to sing my favorite Reggaeton song. The whole bar started to dance and he came singing to me and danced with me!

　　我在哥倫比亞·波哥大拜訪朋友的時候，有一天晚上我們去一個很小的酒吧，台上有一個歌手正在唱著拉丁的情歌。一切看起來都很正常，直到那個歌手走向我的朋友並用西班牙文問他們我喜歡哪一種音樂，我跟他說雷鬼動，也就是我以前很喜歡的很像是西文版的嘻哈音樂。他走回去樂團跟其他樂手說話，然後他就開始唱了我最喜歡的雷鬼

音樂

動的歌。整個酒吧都在跳舞，他還來對我唱歌，並跟我一起跳舞。

Matt
麥特

I was visiting the Finger Lake area and my friends told me about the Flotilla they were doing on one of the finger lake for 4th of July. Everyone took out their boats and tied them together. They had some performers played live music together and just enjoyed a good day on the lake. That was pretty cool for me to see.

　當我獨立紀念日在手指湖的時候，我的朋友跟我說他們在獨立紀念日那天有 Flotilla（小型艦隊）這個活動。大家都把他們的船開出來，然後綁在一起。他們有請一些表演者來表演一些現場音樂，然後就享受那美好的一天。我那時候覺得真的超酷的。

Becca
貝卡

I went to Taiwan and found out this local's favorite

hangout, KTV, which stands for Kareoke Television. You can reserve a room with a big TV screen, and order songs from the computer system and sing them with your friends. It's really fun because you are not singing in front of a bunch of people you don't know. You can order food and drinks, too. I thought that was so cool.

我去台灣的時候發現當地人最喜歡去的地方是 KTV。你可以訂一個包廂，裡面有很大的電視銀幕。你可以從電腦系統裡面點歌，然後跟你的朋友一起唱歌。真的很好玩因為你不是在一群你不認識的人裡面唱歌。你還可以點吃的跟喝的。我覺得很酷。

 Useful expressions

⛵ **take...down memory lane** 帶你回憶

❶ The food here really takes me down memory lane. I remember we ate here a lot when we went to school here.

這裡的食物真的帶我回到回憶裡。我還記得我們在這裡上學的時候很常在這裡吃飯。

⛵ **from time to time** 有的時候

❷ You have to switch up the places to go from time to time. Otherwise, it gets old quickly.

有的時候你應該要換地方去。不然一下子就很無聊了。

音
樂

⛵ go far 有成就，有作為的

❸ This kid is going to go far. He is very talented and he works so hard.

這小孩一定會很有成就的。他很有天份而且有那麼努力的工作。

⛵ fool around 胡鬧

❹ Stop fooling around. We need to finish the work by tonight.

不要再胡鬧了。我們要在今天晚上之前完成這工作。

⛵ jam 即興演奏

❺ Bring your ukulele and let's jam tonight!

今天晚上帶你的烏克麗麗，我們來即興演奏！

⛵ have my doubts 有我的疑慮

❻ I still have my doubts about his products at the beginning, but now I realize it's really good products with great quality.

我一開始對他的產品有一些疑慮，但是我現在知道他的產品很好，品質也很好。

⛵ have goose bumps 起雞皮疙瘩

❼ I had goose bumps when I was watching this movie.

我看這部電影的時候有起了雞皮疙瘩。

⚓ here and there 到處

❽ When you live with girls with long hair, you have to get used to seeing hair here and there.

你跟長頭髮的女生一起住的時候，你就要習慣常常到處都看得到頭髮。

 背景起源

The smell of the candy shop, the cheering words people wish upon each other and just the joyful spirits everyone is showing in the festival are enough to make a festival fun. Festivals are usually celebrations with specific purposes. It could be religious or used as commemoration; the purposes vary in each case. Nevertheless, they could just be the excuses people made up to have fun since what these festivals hold in common is the fact that festivals are always fun-guaranteed. Big feasts, breathtaking fireworks, festive music and dance, and the fun atmosphere are just all over the place. Believe it or not, it would be a challenge not to have fun in festivals.

糖果店裡的味道,大家互相祝福的話語,還有大家高興的精神就已經足夠讓一個節日好玩了!節日通常都是因為慶祝某個原因而誕生,可能是宗教的因素,又或者是用來紀念某一件事;每個節日背後的原因都不大一樣。但是也有可能是大家為了要玩樂所編出來的藉口啦。因為所有節日的共同點就是他們都幾乎是保證好玩的。大餐、令人驚嘆的煙火、節慶的音樂和舞蹈，到處都是的歡樂氣氛。信不信由你，在節慶裡覺得很無聊也是一件很難的事。

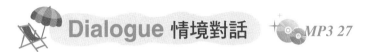

Dialogue 情境對話　MP3 27

Jasmine and Ray are in Buñol, Spain for the Tomato Festival (La Tomatina in Spanish).
潔斯敏和雷在西班牙的布尼奧爾參加蕃茄節。

Jasmine: Oh my god, Ray, I cannot believe how many people there are here.

潔斯敏：我的天啊，雷，我不敢相信有這麼多人在這裡。

Ray: I know, according to the radio we listened to on the way here, there are going to be about 50, 000 participants from all over the world today.

雷：對啊！我們剛剛來的路上聽的電台有說今天會有五萬個從世界各地來參加的人。

Jasmine: I'm so excited about this huge food fight! We should probably buy the goggles and gloves people are selling. That sounds like a good idea.

潔斯敏：我好期待這個超大的食物大戰喔！我們應該要買個這邊在賣的護目鏡和手套。好像是一個還不錯的點子。

Ray: Yeah, I agree with you. Look around us. There are tour buses all over the place. I recognize the Russian and Japanese languages on the buses. This is a bigger event than I imagined it.

雷：對啊，我也這麼覺得。你看看我們週遭到處都有觀光巴士耶。我有認出巴士上的俄文還有另一個是日文。這是一個比我想像還要大很多的活動耶。

Jasmine: I know, right? We should probably head over to the plaza where the festival takes place.

潔斯敏：對啊！我們應該要朝著丟蕃茄的廣場前進了。

Ray: Yeah, we should, if we can pass all these people in front of us.

雷：對啊，我們應該要的，如果我們可以超過我們前面這些人的話。

Jasmine: Look Ray, what's that person doing climbing up the wooden pole up there?

潔斯敏：雷你看！那個人爬上那個木頭的柱子要幹嘛？

Ray: It's the tradition. The festival starts when some brave soul reaches the ham at the top of the greased-up pole. It is very challenging in my opinion.

雷：喔那是傳統啊！如果某個很勇敢的人可以爬上這個抹了油的柱子，然後把上面的火腿拿下來的話，蕃茄節就會正式開始。我覺得超難的。

Jasmine: Well, that's a lot of pressure on him! What happens if no one can do it?

潔斯敏：喔，那對那個人來說壓力好大喔！如果沒人可以做到呢？

Ray: Well, it's only for the entertaining purpose. The festival will start whether anyone reaches the ham or not.

雷：喔其實那只是為了娛樂效果啦！蕃茄節不管有沒有人可以拿得到火腿都會開始啦！

Jasmine: Oh, what a relief. The festival will start in any second now!

潔斯敏：喔，真讓人鬆一口氣。那番茄節就隨時都會開始了耶！

Ray: Make sure you crush your tomatoes before you throw at anyone! And you know what makes it even more fun?

雷：你在丟番茄前一定要先把番茄捏碎喔！而且你知道怎麼樣會更好玩嗎？

Jasmine: What?

潔斯敏：怎麼樣？

Ray: If you just secretly aim at the same person the whole time...

雷：如果你一直偷偷瞄準同一個人丟的話⋯

節日慶典

01
Question

Do you enjoy festivals? Why? Why not?
你喜歡節慶嘛？為什麼喜歡或是為什麼不喜歡？

Michelle
蜜雪兒

I'm not a festival person per say. I don't think I like it that much mainly because of the crowds a festival brings. If people can just keep a safe distance and mind their own business, then I might be fine with it, but that's not usually the case. Too many people just make everything worse. The traffic is bad, the bathrooms are dirty, and people get injured all the time in a festival. I'd rather stay at home and watch TV I think.

　　我本身沒有很喜歡節慶啦。我覺得我不喜歡的原因主要是因為節慶都會有很多人。如果大家可以保持安全距離，或是只管他們自己的閒事的話，那我就還可以參加，可是通常都不是那樣。人太多就會把一切搞砸。交通會很塞，廁所會變得很髒，很多人參加慶典也都會受傷。我覺得我寧願在家看電視。

Matt
麥特

I'm all about it. I love everything about a festival. The smell, the people, the music, the food, and the dance...I can go on and on about this all day. I always feel so alive when I'm in one of those events. It makes me feel like I'm a little kid again, and it's okay, too. Love it.

我最喜歡節慶了！我喜歡關於節慶的每一件事。節慶的味道、人群、音樂、食物和跳舞…我可以一直說下去。我每次參加這類的活動時就會覺得我是活著的。它讓我覺得我好像又變成一個小孩子，而且那樣也沒關係。超棒的。

Becca
貝卡

You know, I've been there and done that. I think it's cool to check it out, but I'm just over the party scenes. I'm at that age where most of my friends hang out at the coffee shops instead of clubs. I guess I'm just having the quarter life crisis. Haha... I'm usually ready to go to bed when it hits

節日慶典

10:30. I guess if the festivals are in the daytime, I want to check it out, but if not, I won't cry my heart out.

你知道，我已經做過那些事了。我是覺得去看看是不錯，可是我已經不 party 了。我已經到了那個大多數的朋友都會在咖啡店而不是在夜店裡的年紀了。我想我現在應該是有四分之一年危機（25 歲）。哈哈…而且我通常十點半就會去睡了。如果那些節慶是在白天的話，我會去看看，不然沒去的話我也不會傷心的要命啦。

02
Question

What is the most impressive festival you have ever been to?
你去過最令你印象深刻的節慶是什麼？

Michelle
蜜雪兒

I went to the Carnival of Venice, and it was such a gorgeous festival. Everyone dressed up nicely and wore these amazing masks. I had to buy so many of those masks before I left Venice. There were fireworks by the canal, too. Very impressive and when can you dress up like that with so many people anyways?

　　我去了威尼斯的嘉年華會。那個節慶真是超美的。大家都精心打扮然後還帶了很棒的面具。我在離開威尼斯之前不得不買了很多面具。在運河旁也有放煙火。超令人印象深刻的，而且你還可以去哪裡精心打扮成那樣？

Matt
麥特

　　The most impressive festival I've ever been to is the Oktoberfest in Munich. It was a pretty big event, and I always thought Oktoberfest is all about beer drinking, but to my surprise, there are water slides, fun rides, food stands and then there are the big tents for beers and pretzels. It was really fun to see how people dressed in traditional German outfits. I had such a great time there!

　　我去過最令我印象深刻的節慶是在慕尼黑的啤酒節。那是一個蠻大的節慶，而且我一直以為啤酒節就只是喝啤酒而已，可是令我很意外的是那裡有很多滑水道、遊樂設施、食物的攤販。然後你才會看到他們有設立一些大帳篷，裡面你才可以喝啤酒和吃扭結餅。看大家穿著德國傳統的服飾真的很好玩，我玩得超開心的。

節日慶典

Becca
貝卡

I went and celebrated the festival of lights, or Diwali, with my friends in India. It was actually the Hindu New Year, so in a way, it was their New Year celebration. It was really impressive because besides the big fireworks to start with, there were candles everywhere. Every household decorated their houses, too. It was just a very stunning festival to participate.

我在印度跟我的朋友一起慶祝了排燈節，而那時候正是印度教的新年，所以其實也就是他們新年的慶典。那個節慶很令人印象深刻因為除了一開始的時候有盛大的煙火，也有隨處可見的蠟燭。每家每戶也都會佈置他們的房子。那真是一個很美的節日。

03
Question

What is the strangest festival you have ever heard of?
你聽過最奇怪的節慶是什麼呢？

The Songkran Festival in Thailand is pretty bizarre for me. They dump water on each other during the New Year celebration. It's said that they do this to wash away the bad luck or bad spirits away...I think they might have taken that a little too literally.

我覺得泰國的潑水節真的對我來說很奇怪。他們會在新年的時候互相潑彼此水。據說他們是想要潑掉厄運或是邪靈…可是我覺得他們好像真的想得太簡單和直接了。

I heard about this festival in Thailand. It's called the monkey festival. What the locals do is that they lay out the fruits to attract a lot of monkeys. The strange part is that they only do this to boost the tourism. Weird, isn't it?

我聽說在泰國有一個節叫做猴子節。當地人會把很多水果擺出來吸

節日慶典

175

引猴子。我覺得奇怪的點是他這個節日完全只是因為要吸引遊客而產生的。很奇怪吧？

The strangest festival I've heard of is the Day of the Dead that's celebrated in Mexico. At the beginning, it's strange for me that people "celebrate" the fact that their family is dead, but then I thought that is such a good idea. On this day, the families gather together, have fun and share stories about their family that had passed away. A strange but good idea!

我聽過最奇怪的節是墨西哥的亡靈節。一開始的時候我覺得很奇怪，為什麼他們要「慶祝」亡靈，可是我後來覺得這真的是蠻好的點子。在這天，家人會聚在一起玩樂，和互相分享死去的家人故事。很奇怪，但是是個好主意。

Useful expressions

🔺 **keep a safe distance** 保持適當距離

❶ You should keep a safe distance from her. I don't think she's up to anything good.

我覺得你應該要跟她保持距離。我覺得她好像不懷好意。

🔺 **I'm all about it!** 我最喜歡…；全心投入…

❷ You know how I feel about politics. I'm all about it.

你知道我對政治的想法。我最喜歡政治了。

🔺 **been there and done that** 我也經歷過；…已經沒什麼新鮮感了

❸ Her opinion about marriage is "been there and done that." I don't think she will get married again.

她對婚姻的意見是："我竟歷過這件事了。" 我並不覺得她想再婚。

🔺 **cry my heart out** 哭得十分傷心

❹ She cried her heart out the day she broke up with her boyfriend.

她跟她男友分手的那天她哭得十分傷心。

Performance / Shows
表演

 背景起源

When you are traveling, you come across many different forms of performances or shows and then you realize quickly that different cultures enjoy different types of entertainment. Some performances can only be seen at certain places, such as traditional dances or sports games whereas some performances are shown all over the world. From the most iconic performances to a random show you step upon, while walking back to your hotel. They all make some differences for your journey. Remember to learn about different cultures and the stories behind the performances and to enjoy the shows with an open mind.

你在旅行的時候會遇到很多不同形式的表演或是秀，然後你很快就會發現原來不一樣的文化喜歡不一樣的娛樂方式。有的表演是只有在某些地方才看得見，例如傳統的舞蹈或是球賽，但有的表演是在世界各地都看得見的。從最具代表性的表演到你走回飯店不小心看到的表演都會使你的旅程有點不同。記得要試著學習在每個表演背後的文化和故事，還有以開闊的心胸來看表演喔！

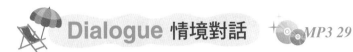 **Dialogue 情境對話** MP3 29

Jake Shimabukuro was touring in Japan. Aaron and his friend Miyu are at his Ukulele concert.

傑克島袋正在日本巡回表演。艾倫和他的朋友成美正在傑克島袋的烏克麗麗音樂會裡。

Aaron: He is one of the best ukulele players I know. I'm really excited we can come to this.	艾倫：他是我知道最厲害的烏克麗麗手之一。我真的很興奮我們可以來這個。
Miyu: Me, too. Luckily we got the tickets. I know a lot of my friends were trying so hard to come, but they couldn't get any tickets.	成美：我也是。我們真的很幸運可以買得到票耶。我知道我有很多朋友超想要來的，可是都買不到票。
Aaron: I didn't realize he's big in Japan, too!	艾倫：我不知道原來他在日本也那麼紅！
Miyu: Yeah, he is! Hey here we go!!!	成美：對啊，他真的很

He's playing!!

紅！欸開始了！他在演奏了！！

Aaron: It's so amazing how fast he's playing the ukulele. I can't even see his fingers.

艾倫：他可以彈烏克麗麗彈得那麼快真的很厲害耶！我都看不到他的手指。

Miyu: I know, and it is so different than the regular ukulele performances. It's like that's coming out from another instrument!

成美：對啊，而且他跟一般的烏克麗麗表演差好多喔。好像他在彈不一樣的樂器一樣。

Aaron: Yes, his strumming is so energetic and powerful. I wish I could play like him.

艾倫：對啊，他的彈奏真的好有活力又很有力。我真希望我可以彈得跟他一樣。

Miyu: I just wish I could even play anything.

成美：我只希望我會彈就好了。

Aaron: Well, that's not hard, is it? There are a lot of places offering lessons.

艾倫：嗯，那不難吧？現在有很多地方都可以上課啊！

Miyu: You're right, maybe I should

成美：你說的對啦，或

take a lesson and give it a shot.

許我該去上個課試試看。

Aasron: You should, and then maybe you can take me on your tours around the world.

艾倫：你應該要去學的，說不定以後你就可以帶我到處去你的世界巡迴演出。

Miyu: Haha...thanks for the pep talk. But it's going to be a long wait. I'm not the brightest when it comes to music.

成美：哈哈…謝謝你的鼓勵啊！不過你可能要等很久。我沒有什麼音樂細胞。

Aaron: Well...you've got to start somewhere, right?

艾倫：嗯嗯…不過還是得從哪裡開始啊，對吧？

Miyu: True that. Now can we enjoy the show, my life coach?

成美：你說的對啦。那我們現在可不可以開始享受這個表演啊，人生導師？

Aaron: Yes, ma'am.

艾倫：是的，小姐。

01 Question

What type of performances or shows do you enjoy? Why?

你喜歡哪一種表演或是秀呢？為什麼？

Michelle
蜜雪兒

I love going to the magic and acrobatic shows. It just never gets old for me. I love it ever since I was little and I still do. Without those performances and performers, this world is going to be so dull. There is always a joyful atmosphere and full of surprises in those performances, and I guess that's why I love it.

我最喜歡魔術或是雜耍的表演。我都看不膩那些。而且我從小就很喜歡看那些表演。我覺得如果沒有那些表演和表演者的話，這個世界會變得很乏味。在那些表演中總是有很歡樂的氣氛而且也充滿了驚喜。我想那就是為什麼我喜歡它們的原因了。

Matt
麥特

I think the best kind of performances usually comes from the street. There are so many street artists on the road, and many of them are truly talented. They rely the least on other equipment, too. Also, it's the easiest way to engage in a performance, and also to leave one if you don't enjoy them. I think they are the hidden gems of performances.

我覺得最好的表演通常都來自街上。在街上有那麼多的街頭藝人，而且其實他們很多人都真的很有才華！他們也是仰賴任何其他的配備最少的人。另外，我覺得看街頭表演是最容易加入的一種表演，還有如果你不喜歡的話，也是最容易離開的。我個人認為那是表演裡的隱藏珍寶！

Becca
貝卡

I really enjoy musicals. It's live concert mixed with drama and great choreography, too. Musicals are great treats to all our senses. Those performers can do pretty

much everything, and they have not failed me so far. A lot is going on when you are watching a musical. I love it. It is like a combination of birthday party and Christmas.

我最喜歡歌舞劇。因為它就是現場演唱會，加上戲劇和超棒的編舞啊！音樂劇對我們的感官是極大的享受。那些表演者真的什麼都可以表演的出來，而且他們目前為止也沒有讓我失望。在看舞台劇的時候會覺得那個表演很豐富。我超愛的，就像是生日舞會加上聖誕節一樣。

02 Question
Which performance would you recommend to your friends? Why?
你會推薦給你的朋友哪一個表演？為什麼？

Michelle
蜜雪兒

I told every one of my friends that if they are going to Venice, they should stop by Musica a palazzo for a small-scale opera experience. I've been to many different operas. However, to my surprise, Musica a palazzo offers no more than 70 seats. It's tiny, but it also means you are very close to the stage. As a matter of fact, sometimes you are part of

表演

the stage! I think everyone should go there at least once in their lives.

　　我跟我每一個朋友說過如果他們有去威尼斯的話，一定要去 Musica a palazzo 體驗小型的歌劇表演。我有去過很多不一樣的歌劇表演，可是讓我驚訝的是 Musica a palazzo 只有提供不超過七十個座位的表演。那裡很小，但是那也表示你也離舞台很接近。事實上，你有的時候還是舞台的一部分咧！我覺得每個人一生至少要去一次！

Matt
麥特

　　Cirque du Soleil always guarantees great performances and shows. I went to every one of their shows, and I recommended all of them to my friends. It's just amazing to see how professional the whole crew is. It makes me nervous to watch them sometimes, but the performances are just very stunning and artistic ones. They are just too good to pass!

　　太陽劇團永遠都保證有最棒的表演還有秀。我去了他們每一個表演，我也推薦我的朋友去看每一個。你會很傻眼怎麼每一個表演者都那麼專業。有的時候看他們表演我會覺得很緊張，但是整個表演總是那麼美麗跟藝術。他們的表演實在是太好看了，一定不能錯過！

Becca
貝卡

This might sound childish, but it actually isn't. I would recommend Lion King Broadway show to all my friends. At first I thought to myself that nothing is going to beat the original animation, but the show actually pulls it off! The live music, the dance, the visual effects on stage is more than perfect.

聽起來可能會很幼稚，但是它其實一點也不幼稚。我會推薦獅子王百老匯給我所有的朋友。一開始看之前我就想說怎麼可能可以打敗原版動畫獅子王，可是他們真的做到了！現場的音樂、舞蹈和台上的視覺效果都超完美的！

03 Question

Have you been to any one-of-a kind performance? Where was it?
你有去過哪一個獨一無二的表演呢？那是在哪裡？

Michelle
蜜雪兒

When I went to my sister's graduation in Hawaii, we went to the Polynesian Cultural Center, and we watched the night performance that consisted of all different tribes of people in Hawaii. There were Hawaiian, Tahitian, Samoan, Tong Ga...etc. And the show was fantastic, and I don't think I would be able to see it anywhere else.

我去夏威夷參加我妹妹的畢業典禮時，我們去了波里尼西亞文化中心看了一個在晚上的表演。它綜合了夏威夷各族人。有夏威夷人、大溪地人、薩摩爾和東加…等等。那個秀真的棒透了，而我也覺得那是在別的地方看不到的表演。

Matt
麥特

I was once traveling in Manhattan and of course I had to check out Time Square. Just when I was taking some pictures there, there was one guy started singing "just the way you are" by Bruno Mars, and then more people joined

him and they all started dancing. I quickly realized they are the flash mobs! I recorded the whole thing right away. After they finished, everyone cheered and they went different directions. I thought that I was so lucky.

我在曼哈頓旅行的時候，當然得去時代廣場看看。就在我在那裡照相的時候，突然有個男的開始唱火星人布魯諾的 "Just the way you are"，然後越來越多人加入他唱歌和跳舞。我馬上就想到他們就是快閃族！我立刻全程錄影。他們結束後，大家就歡呼，然後他們就往不同的方向離開了。我那時候覺得我真的超幸運的！

Becca
貝卡

I went to an impromptu comedy when I was in Amsterdam. Usually, I go to the standup comedy show, but rarely do I go to the impromptu comedies. What it was was that they improvised the show as they go. Usually they perform the interaction between them and the audience. There was no script. I thought that was really impressive and literally one-of-a-kind!

我去了阿姆斯特丹的即興喜劇表演。我通常都只是去喜劇表演，超少去即興喜劇表演。那其實就是他們全程都是即興表演。通常是從跟觀眾或是他們自己本身的互動中延伸出來的。完全沒有劇本。我覺得那是很令人印象深刻還有真的是獨一無二的表演。

 Useful expressions

⛵ **give it a shot 試試看**

❶ I know it's not going to be easy, but I want to give it a shot.

我知道這並不會很簡單，但是我還是想要試試看。

⛵ **pep talk 精神喊話，鼓勵**

❷ The coach gave everyone a pep talk before the game started.

教練在比賽之前給大大家一個精神喊話。

⛵ **one of a kind 獨一無二的**

❸ For every parent, his or her kids are all one of a kind.

對每一個家長來說，他們的小孩都是獨一無二的。

16
Unit

Amusement Park
遊樂園

 背景起源

Amusement parks always <u>hold a very special place in our hearts</u>. It's a place filled with joy, laughter, excitement, ice creams and slurpees. Just like its name, you go there to get amused and entertained. There are all sorts of rides and facilities in the park for people to enjoy. This is the place where your wildest imagination comes true and so do your worst nightmares sometimes. This is the place where Harry Potter meets Roller Coasters and Mickey Mouse comes to shake your hands in the heat-stroke prone outfit. It sounds dreamy, but another feature of the amusement parks is the long lines. Expect to wait in lines, and stay hydrated! Buckle up and have fun!

遊樂園在我們的心中都有一個很特別的地位。那是一個充滿了快樂、歡笑、刺激、冰淇淋還有思樂冰的地方。就像它的名字一樣，你就是去那裡遊樂，還有被娛樂的。那裡有各種不同的遊樂和園區設施你可以使用。這是一個你最狂野的想像或是有的時候最恐怖的噩夢成真的地方。這裡也是哈利波特遇到雲霄飛車，還有米奇老鼠穿著可能會中暑的衣服來跟你握手的地方。聽起來很夢幻，可是遊樂園另一個特色就是排隊。所以預期要排隊，然後要多喝水！繫好安全帶玩得愉快！

Dialogue 情境對話　MP3 31

Summer and Royce are at Disney Land in Los Angeles.
夏天和羅伊斯正在洛杉磯的迪士尼樂園。

Royce: It just amazes me that there are so many people in Disney Land.

羅伊斯：迪士尼樂園有這麼多人真是令我傻眼。

Summer: It is Disney Land you are talking about. What do you expect? That everyone hates Mickey Mouse and Frozen?

夏天：畢竟你說的是迪士尼樂園啊！不然你以為是怎麼樣？大家都恨米奇老鼠還有冰雪奇緣嗎？

Royce: I get your points, but I can't help but wonder how much Disney Land is making.

羅伊斯：我知道你的意思，但我只是無法想像迪士尼可以賺多少錢。

Summer: The tickets are so pricy, too.

夏天：票也超貴的。現

遊樂園

Dreams are not cheap nowadays.

在買一個想真的不便宜。

Royce: No, they aren't. Well, where do you want to go? It looks like we have to wait for a long time anywhere we go anyways, so just pick one.

羅伊斯：真的不便宜。嗯，你想要去哪裡啊？看來到處都要排很久的樣子，所以隨便你選一個吧。

Summer: Follow me, Royce. Let's go find the fast pass machine and get the fast passes.

夏天：跟我走，羅伊斯。我們去找快速通行卡的機器，然後拿快速通行卡。

Royce: What are those for? I thought we already got tickets?

羅伊斯：那是要幹嘛的？我以為我們已經買好票了？

Summer: It's pretty much a ticket that puts us in line. There will be a return time, and we just have to come back at the time the ticket indicates. We can skip the whole waiting process. At least the very long waits anyways.

夏天：其實就是一個幫我們排隊的票啦。上面會有一個叫我們什麼時候回來的時間，然後我們就只要在票叫我們回來的時間回來就好了。我們可以跳過整個排隊的過程。至少跳過那些等很久的啦。

Royce: That's genius. We just have to get all the fast passes and figure out where to go first then.

羅伊斯：好聰明喔。所以我們就只要去拿那些快速通行卡，然後再看要先去哪一個就好了。

Summer: Yep, it's simple as that. It's amazing how much time you can actually save.

夏天：對啊，就是那麼簡單。你會很驚訝我們可以省下多少時間。

Royce: I'm surprised not more people know about this.

羅伊斯：我很驚訝沒有更多人知道這東西。

Summer: Hurray for us!

夏天：對我們來說超棒的啊！

 三問三答　 MP3 32

01 Question

What is your favorite amusement park?

你最喜歡哪一間遊樂園？

 Michelle
蜜雪兒

Disneyland!! It is just the best amusement ever. I've been to almost all the Disneyland in the world, and I can't say I like any particular one. They are all unique in their own ways. Who doesn't like Disney Land really? Cinderella's castle, the carousel, and all the magic in the park. It feels like a dream come true when I'm in Disney Land.

迪士尼樂園！它就是最棒的遊樂園啊！我幾乎去遍全世界所有的迪士尼樂園，但是我說不出來我最喜歡哪一個。它們都有自己獨特的地方。不過說真的怎麼可能會有人不喜歡迪士尼樂園？仙杜瑞拉的城堡、旋轉木馬還有園內所有的魔法。在迪士尼樂園裡就好像是夢想成真一樣！

Matt
麥特

My favorite amusement park is actually a water park called Schlitterbahn. It <u>hands down</u> the best amusement park in the world. The countless water slides are all very long and fun. You can carry the tubes around the park to do all kinds of slides or just float around the floating river. There are always long lines, but no one seems to care too much once they get on the ride.

我最喜歡的遊樂園其實是一間叫做 Schlitterbahn 的水上樂園。它真的是我認為世界上最棒的遊樂園。數不清的滑水道都很長又很好玩。你在園內也都可以拿著游泳圈去各式各樣的滑水道，或是只是在漂漂河上漂。雖然都要排隊很久，但是大家都是坐到之後就不會在意了。

Becca
貝卡

The Universal's Islands of adventures in Orlando! It's both intriguing and exciting. Once you graduate from Disney Land, you would enjoy this place so much. I only spent one

day there, and I couldn't finish trying all the rides and exploring the park fully. I was <u>in tears</u> when I needed to leave. I even swore I'd be back one day! It's still on my to-do list!

在奧蘭多的環球影城冒險島樂園！它又好玩又刺激。你在迪士尼樂園畢業之後，你就會很喜歡這個地方。我只有在那裡玩一天，可是我沒有試過全部的設施也沒有探索完整個園區。我是含淚離開那個地方的。我還發誓我有一天一定會再回來玩的！現在那個還在我要做的事情的清單上面。

02
Question

What was your worst experience in the amusement park?
你在遊樂園裡最糟的經驗是什麼？

Michelle
蜜雪兒

I would dedicate my worst experience to the Haunted House at L.A. Universal Studio. Their problem was that they took everything way too seriously. It was a walking tour through the whole haunted house. Everything in the haunted house was as if they came out directly from the <u>crime scene</u>. I had nightmares and was scarred to go to any haunted house after that one.

　　我要把我在遊樂園最糟的經驗頒給在洛杉磯環球影城的鬼屋。他們的問題就是他們太認真了啦。那是一個要走路穿過鬼屋的行程。每一個在那個鬼屋裡面的東西都好像是直接從犯罪現場搬來的。我再去玩那個鬼屋之後就做惡夢，而且還從此對鬼屋有陰影。

Matt
麥特

I've never really had a bad experience in the amusement park although there was one time when we were stuck on the Ferris wheel for an hour. I didn't mind it, but it gets scary because we didn't know when we could get back to the ground. It was pretty windy up there, too. Then, I started to have flashbacks about those horrifying scenes from the scary movies.

　　我在遊樂園裡沒有什麼不好的經驗，不過有一次我在摩天輪上面卡了一個小時。我一開始是不介意，但是後來越來越可怕因為我們不知道什麼時候才可以回到陸地上。而且在上面的時候風也很大。然後我腦海

就開始有一些恐怖片裡面的恐怖情節畫面。

Becca
貝卡

My worst experience was actually kind of funny. I got motion sickness when I was on a roller coaster ride. My best friend at the time was nice enough to sit me down at the chair nearby and listened to how dizzy I felt the whole time. To my surprise, she was the one that puked at the end. I felt very bad for her, but wasn't I the sick one?

我最不好的經驗其實還蠻好笑的。我坐完雲霄飛車的時候開始有點暈。我那時候最好的朋友人很好的帶我去坐在附近的椅子上，而且還全程一直聽我說我有多暈。嚇到我的是，後來是她在吐。我覺得蠻對不起她的，可是我才是不舒服的人，不是嗎？

03
Question

Do you prefer to ride at the front or at the back of a rollercoaster? Why?
你坐雲霄飛車的時候比較喜歡坐在哪裡？為什麼？

Michelle
蜜雪兒

I prefer to sit in the middle because the ride is smoother in the middle. I'm not too crazy about rollercoasters, but I am usually not in the mood to fight for the front or back seats really. The wait at the line is long enough, so I usually just want to get on the ride when it's my turn.

我比較喜歡坐在中間，因為在中間的時候坐起來比較順。我是沒有很喜歡雲霄飛車啦，所以通常我都沒什麼興趣跟大家爭坐在最前面或是最後面。排隊的時候已經等了夠久了，所以到我的時候我只想趕快坐上去。

Matt
麥特

I love to sit at the back! People always think it's more exciting to sit at the front when you are on a rollercoaster ride, but the truth is quite the opposite. The train accelerates when it's going down, and it's faster to sit at the back sit. Try it next time and see it yourself!

　　我喜歡坐在後面！大家都會以為在雲霄飛車上面要坐在前面比較刺激，可是其實事實是相反的。列車會在下降的時候加速，而且坐在後面比較快。下次你自己試試看！

Becca
貝卡

I prefer to sit at the front seat. My rationale is if I've decided to go on the ride and I paid for the ride, I'm gonna get on the best seat possible. The front row for me is the best because of its view and no one is in front of you, which gives you no warning about what's coming up next! It gives me chills just thinking about it.

　　我比較喜歡坐在前排。我的邏輯是如果我已經決定要坐雲霄飛車了，而且我還花了錢，那我就一定要坐在最好的位置。對我來說坐在前排是最好的位置因為你的前面沒有人，風景比較好。而且也沒有人可以警告你接下來會發生什麼事！我想到就不寒而慄。

Useful expressions

⛵ **hold a special place in one's heart** 在某人的心中有很特別的位置

❶ The cat holds a very special place in her heart.

那隻貓在她的心目中有很特別的位置。

⛵ **a dream come true** 夢想成真

❷ Going to Paris is like a dream come true. I still can't believe it.

可以去巴黎真的是夢想成真。我現在還無法想像。

⛵ **hands down** 無疑的

❸ The food at this place hands down the best.

這個地方的食物無疑是最棒的！

⛵ **in tears** 含淚

❹ She was speaking in tears on stage. Everyone was very moved by her speech.

她在台上是含淚在演講。大家都被她的演說感動。

⛵ **crime scene** 犯罪現場

❺ What happened to this place? It's like a crime scene.

這裡發生什麼事啊？怎麼好像犯罪現場一樣。

17 Cruises
遊輪

 背景起源

Imagine there is way of travel with which you can travel to different countries but stay in the same room. All the visas are taken care of, and the meals are all included. What's more, there are all kinds of entertainment for you to enjoy when you are on board. What am I referring to? Cruises of course! Being on a cruise is many people's dream. They can live on a boat comfortably and travel to different countries this way. It's vacation all the way. There is no waste of your vacation time. Picking your own route and favorite destinations are possible nowadays. However, make sure you wash your hands and look out for stomach flu. You don't want to be a killjoy of everyone's trip!

想像看看有一種旅遊方式是可以讓你到很多個國家旅行，但是你都是住同一個房間。所有的簽證都處理好了，而且餐點也都有包括。還有什麼呢？你在船上的時候有各種娛樂供你選擇。我是在說什麼呢？當然是遊輪囉！去坐遊輪一直都是很多人的夢想。他們可以在一個船上舒服的旅行到不一樣的國家。全程都是度假。完全不浪費你的假期。現在你也可以選擇你自己的路線還有最喜歡的目的地。但是，要確保你洗手，並且小心腸病毒。你不想要掃大家的興的！

 **Dialogue 情境對話** *MP3 33*

Brent and Rochelle are on the Disney Cruise from Florida to Mexico.
布蘭特和若雪兒正在從佛羅里達出發要到邁阿密的迪士尼遊輪上。

Rochelle: Thank you so much for agreeing to come to this with me!	若雪兒：謝謝你願意跟我一起來！
Brent: This is actually really fun. The AquaDuck Water Coaster is so fun!! At one point the slide even goes out of the ship! I'm really impressed.	布蘭特：這裡其實還蠻好玩的。那個超級滑水梯超好玩的！而且它中間有某一段甚至還超出了船身！我覺得蠻厲害的。
Rochelle: See, I told you it won't be that bad!	若雪兒：看吧！我就跟你說沒那麼糟了！
Brent: Hey don't <u>push it</u>! I said it's	布蘭特：欸欸不要得寸

fun already. You do notice that we are the only adults without kids here.

進尺喔！我就說很厲害了。你有注意到我們是唯一沒有帶小孩來的大人。

Rochelle: We think young! Should we go try how to edit and produce a film? Who knows, maybe we can make the next best Disney movie!

若雪兒：我們是思想年輕！我們要不要去試試看編輯製作一部片？誰知道，我們可能會作出迪士尼下一個大作耶！

Brent: Yep, we like to think positively, too! I hate to admit it, but I kind of enjoy this.

布蘭特：對啊，我們思想也很樂觀。我是很不想承認，可是我還蠻喜歡這的。

Rochelle: Just to be fair, we can go grab a drink at the bar later.

若雪兒：公平起見，我們等下可以去酒吧喝一杯。

Brent: Oh wow, who is the grown up here? I almost forgot she came to this cruise with me, too!

布蘭特：哇賽！這個大人是誰？我都忘了她也有跟我來這個遊輪。

Rochelle: I should probably change my mind.

若雪兒：還是我應該要改變主意。

Brent: No, you shouldn't. That was a brilliant idea! Good job Rochelle! I'm proud of you! Now let's make some film and go grab a drink afterwards.

布蘭特：不用，你不應該要改變主意。那是一個超棒的主意。做得好若雪兒！我好驕傲喔！現在我們去製片，然後去喝一杯吧！

Rochelle: You're the best!

若雪兒：你最好了！

Brent: I don't know what you're talking about!

布蘭特：我不知道你在說什麼！

遊輪

三問三答　MP3 34

01 Question

Have you ever been on any cruise? How was it?
你有搭過遊輪嗎？結果怎麼樣？

Michelle
蜜雪兒

I was on a cruise for a friend's wedding. Their wedding was a destination wedding, and the ship took everyone to

Hawaii and that's where my friends had the ceremony. It was a perfect way to get everyone together and celebrate their wedding together. It was the best wedding party I've ever been to. However, I have to say that perhaps there is a reason why normally the wedding is only 1 day! I can't handle partying for a week! It's just too much.

　　我有在遊輪上面慶祝我朋友的婚禮。他們的婚禮是一個度假婚禮。遊輪帶大家去夏威夷參加他們的結婚典禮。那是一個很完美的辦法把大家聚在一起，並且一起慶祝他們的婚禮。那是我去過最棒的婚禮，可是我必須說或許一般的婚禮都只有一天是有原因的！我實在是沒有辦法狂歡一個禮拜！太累了啦！

Matt
麥特

　　I have a buddy who works for a cruise ship, so he pulled some string and got me a ticket to a short cruise to Alaska. It was so nice and the cruise was beautiful. When we got to Alaska, we even went sports fishing. I had a blast and even if half of the time I was seasick, it was still a great experience.

　　我有一個好朋友在遊輪上工作，於是他就動用了一些關係幫我拿到一張短程去阿拉斯加的遊輪。整個旅程很好而且那段路也十分的美麗。當我們到阿拉斯加的時候，我們還去釣魚。即使一半的行程我都在暈船，我還是玩得很開心。那是一個很棒的經驗。

Becca
貝卡

　　I went on a sunset cruise at the Darling Harbour at Sydney. It was really romantic and the sunset was beautiful. I did notice there were a lot of couples, and so it was a little bit weird. Other than that, the food is great, and they also have drinks on board, too. It was really nice to tour around Darling Harbour and frankly I think that's the best way!

　　我在雪梨的時候去了達令港坐日落遊輪。我覺得很浪漫而且日落也好美。我的確是有注意到很多的情侶，所以那有點奇怪。除了那樣之外，食物很好吃，而且他們船上也有喝的。我覺得用遊輪觀光達令港是一個蠻棒的方式，老實說，我覺得是最棒的方式。

02 Question

Do you get seasick easily?
你會很容易暈船嗎？

Michelle
蜜雪兒

To my surprise, not really. I'm actually pretty good with it. So far I haven't got seasick from the cruises. I'm <u>born to</u> do this I guess. There were times when the water was rougher than it should have been, and many people got sick. I was still in good shape though. It's pretty amazing.

很令我驚訝，可是我不太會暈船耶。而且其實我還蠻厲害的。到目前為止我在遊輪上都沒有暈船過。我想我就是生下來要坐遊輪的。而且有的時候海浪真的超大的，然後很多人都暈了，可是我還是很好。還蠻令人驚訝的。

Matt
麥特

遊輪

Scarily yes. I've tried everything, but I think I just get motion sickness easily. I get car sick, seasick, and I even get sick when I'm on the plane. But I still <u>can't pass traveling up</u> though. Oh and by the way, the wristband that's supposed to help you with seasickness doesn't work!

超容易的。我試過每個東西，可是我覺得我就是很容易暈的人。我會暈車、暈船，坐飛機我也會暈。但是我還是不能放棄旅行啦。喔對了，那個手腕上在戴的防暈手環，完全沒用！

Becca
貝卡

<u>It depends</u>. If I have enough sleep and I have something in my stomach, I'm usually fine. Nevertheless, I had really bad experiences when I got seasick on a sailboat. Once I was on a boat. Everything was fine until I went into the tiny bathroom on the boat, and then everything <u>went downhill</u> from there.

要看情況耶。如果我有睡得飽，然後也有吃點東西的話，我通常都還好。但是我也有暈船很嚴重的經驗。有一次我在船上。本來都好好的直到我去一間很小間的廁所上廁所，然後我就開始走下坡了。

03 **Question**

Rumor has it that an average person gains five pounds of a one-week cruise, do you think it's true?

有謠言說一個正常的人搭一個禮拜的遊輪，大約會胖個 2.3 公斤左右。你覺得是真的嗎？

Michelle
蜜雪兒

<u>I can see that happen</u> because it's like a week of vacation when you are on the cruise. People usually gain weight when they are on vacation, right? You eat, you drink and you read a novel and chill. Forget about working hard to maintain your goal weight. We deserve it. Isn't that how it works?

我覺得有可能因為在遊輪上就好像是你度了一個禮拜的假啊！大家在度假的時候不是都會變胖嗎？你吃東西、喝東西，然後你看本小書放鬆一下。努力運動保持理想的體重都已經在九霄雲外了。我們值得享受一下。這不是都是這樣嗎？

I think gaining weight is a personal choice. There are still all kinds of workout facilities on the boat. There is even a swimming pool if you want to swim. And I guess it also depends on what kind of food they are serving and how often you eat. Like I said, personal choices.

我覺得變胖是個人選擇。而且在遊輪上面也都有各式各樣健身的器材。如果你想要游泳的話，有的還甚至是有游泳池耶。不過我想也是看他們都是上怎麼樣的菜，還有你多常去吃。就像我說的，個人選擇啦！

Totally. When I'm on the cruise, I'm really trying to make it worth it. I eat and drink the complementary ones as much as possible, and by the way, they are not complimentary. I paid to get in. Also, sometimes it's nice to splurge a little when you are on vacation. When you can't fit in your jeans anymore, wear a dress!

　　當然！我在遊輪上的時候，我是真的想要讓它值回票價。我會盡可能多吃那些招待的食物和飲料，不過順帶一提，那些並不是招待的。我是有買票進來的。還有啦，有的時候度假時揮霍一下也不錯啦。當你穿不下你的牛仔褲時穿洋裝。

 **Useful expressions**

⛵ **killjoy** 掃興的人，煞風景

❶ Don't invite her to the party. She's such a killjoy!

不要邀請她來派對啦，她真的很掃興耶！

⛵ **push it** 得寸進尺

❷ The salary is good enough. You don't want to push it now.

薪水這樣已經很好了。你這時候不應該得寸進尺。

⛵ **born to** 生下來做…

❸ He is born to be a musician. He is so talented!

他生下來就是要做音樂人的。他那麼有才華！

⛵ **can't pass something up** 不能放棄…

❹ I just couldn't pass that concert up! I had to drive all the way home for that.

我就是不能錯過那個演唱會！我就是一定得開這麼遠的車回來。

⚓ It depends 看情況

❺ My boss asked me how fast I could finish the work today. How do I know? It depends.

我的老闆今天問我我多快可以完成工作。我怎麼知道啊？要看情況啊。

⚓ go downhill 走下坡

❻ I think the restaurant is going downhill ever since someone got food poisoned last time.

我覺得這家餐廳自從上次讓一個客人食物中毒之後就開始走下坡了。

⚓ I can see that happen 我覺得很有可能

❼ I think they are going to get married soon. I can see that happen!

我覺得他們很快就會結婚了。我覺得非常有可能。

⚓ Totally 當然

❽ A: Would you like to grab something to eat together?

B: Totally!

A：你想要一起去吃點東西嗎？

B：當然好！

Outfits & Traditional Costumes

Unit 服裝和傳統服飾

 背景起源

It is very interesting to do <u>people watching</u> when you are in a different country. The way people dress represents their identity or who they are as a part of that city. We all know there are roughly two kinds of outfits in every country; formal ones and the casual ones. However, each country has their own definition of what "formal" is. What might be acceptable in one country might not be appropriate in another. Also, each country has their own styles. It's very easy to tell people apart once you <u>get the hang of it.</u> In addition, there are also traditional costumes. In most cases, traditional costumes are used for festivals or as everyday wear. Which one is your favorite?

　　當你在國外時觀察周遭的人其實很有趣。人們穿著的方式代表了他們的身份，或是在這個城市的一份子。我們都知道其實每個國家的服裝都可以大略的歸為兩種：正式和休閒。但是每個國家對於正式的定義也很不同。在這個國家可以接受的服裝，在別的國家可能會很不適當。還有就是，每個國家也都有他們自己的風格。其實你抓到訣竅之後，很好分別大家從哪裡來的。除此之外，還有傳統服飾。大部分來說傳統服飾可以分為在慶典或是每天生活中穿的兩種。你最喜歡哪一種傳統服飾呢？

Dialogue 情境對話 MP3 35

Jean and her friend Barbara are at a Geisha makeover studio in Kyoto.
珍和她的朋友芭芭拉在京都一間藝妓藝廊裡改裝變身中。

Jean: Wow, I'm so excited that we get to do this!	珍：哇，我好興奮我們可以來做這個行程喔！
Barbara: I know, this would be something different and definitely unique to do while we are here. You asked me about traditional costumes here the other day, so I had this idea!	芭芭拉：對啊！這會是不一樣的經驗而且也一定會是我們在這裡很獨特的經驗。你前幾天不是在問我關於傳統服飾的問題，我是從那裡得到靈感要做這個的！
Jean: I love it. So wait, how long does the makeover take? I'm just	珍：我超愛的。欸等一下，所以這個改裝要多

trying to think if it's worth the money.

久啊？我只是要想看看這樣錢划不划算。

Barbara: It'll take about 2 hours they said. And then we have photo-shoots with the local professional photographer here.

芭芭拉：他們説會花大約兩個小時的時間，然後當地的一些專業攝影師會幫我們拍一些照。

Jean: 2 hours just for putting on the make up and dress? That's crazy!

珍：兩個小時只是在化妝跟穿衣服？好誇張！

Barbara: Yeah, I don't think the photo shoots will take long at all though.

芭芭拉：對啊，不過我不覺得拍照會花很久的時間。

Jean: I hope not, but oh well, then we'll get a sense of how it is to be a real Geisha.

珍：我希望不會，但是，我們會知道真正當一個藝妓是什麼感覺。

Barbara: Can you imagine the amount of makeup they are going to put on our face though? We're gonna be completely white!

芭芭拉：你可以想像他們要在我們臉上化多少妝嗎？我們會變超白的。

Jean: Oh this is going to be great! I'm definitely going to take some

珍：喔，這一定會很好玩！我一定要拍一些好

funny photos.

笑的照片。

Barbara: Let's do a <u>talent show</u>, too. I'll videotape it. It'll be so fun!

芭芭拉：我們來做才藝表演啦！我來錄影！一定會很好玩！

Jean: A talent show. Hold on a minute. This is getting complicated.

珍：才藝表演。等下，這怎麼變得越來越複雜了。

三問三答　+ MP3 36

Which traditional costumes would you like to try on? Why?

01 Question

世界上所有的傳統服飾裡你有想要試穿哪一個嗎？為什麼？

Michelle
蜜雪兒

I would love to try on the Flamenco dresses from Andalucía, Spain. They are just so bright-colored and passionate. I saw a few Flamenco dancers performing at the mall, and I thought their costumes are so beautiful. Hey,

you know what? I'm gonna be a Flamenco Dancer this Halloween! Thanks for the inspiration! I think I can <u>rock</u> the outfit!

我會想要試試看西班牙安達魯西亞的佛朗明哥裙。它們是那麼的鮮艷和熱情。我有在購物中心看過一些佛朗明歌舞者表演，然後我就在想他們的服裝都好美喔！喔你知道怎樣嗎？我今年的萬聖節要打扮成佛朗明哥舞者！謝謝你給我的靈感！我覺得我一定可以穿得很好看的！

Matt
麥特

I want to try on the Kilts from Scotland! Honestly I've never tried on a skirt in my life. When I first heard about the costume, my friends and I thought that was so ridiculous. Why do men in Scotland wear skirts? However, just because of that, I really want to try it so that I can say I've tried on a Kilt before. And I'm curious about how it feels to be in a skirt. Must be pretty breezy...

我想要試試看蘇格蘭的蘇格蘭裙！老實說，我從來都沒穿過裙子。一開始聽到蘇格蘭裙的時候，我跟我的朋友就想說那真是太荒謬了。蘇格蘭的男人怎麼會穿裙子啊？但是也是因為那樣，我真的很想要試試看，然後我就可以說我有穿過蘇格蘭裙了。而且其實我很好奇穿裙子是什麼感覺。一定很涼⋯

Becca
貝卡

I was in Indian, but I didn't get to try on the Sari there. I did go to the markets, and there are a lot of Sari shops there, and may I just say that the Saris are gorgeous! You can even <u>mix and match</u> your own fabric! I was in a hurry, so I didn't get to try on anything, but if I could <u>go back in time</u>, I would totally try it on!

我有去印度，可是我沒有試穿到紗麗。我有去那裡的市集，那裡有很多賣紗麗的店，而且我可以說紗麗真的是很美嘛！你還可以混搭不同的布料來做你的紗麗！我那時候很趕，所以我不能試穿任何一個，可是如果我可以回到當時的話，我一定會試穿的！

Have you ever felt like you need to change the way you dress when you travel?

你有沒有曾經在旅行的時候覺得你應該要改變你打扮的方式？

Michelle
蜜雪兒

When I was in Milan last year, the first day I was there, I felt like I needed a <u>makeover</u> ASAP! That was the only day I dressed down, and that was the worst experience I've ever had. Everyone was so fashionable on the street. I almost mistaken that I was on the runway. I was wearing a pair of flats! Flats! And I'm so tiny! Arg, so yeah, that was the time I felt like I should change the way I dressed.

我去年在米蘭的時候，第一天到的時候，我覺得我立刻需要一個大改造。而且那是我唯一一天沒什麼打扮，然後那就變成我最糟的經驗了。每個在街上的人都超時尚的。我差點以為我是在參展台上。我那時候正好穿了一雙平底鞋！平底鞋耶！我那麼小隻！哎！所以那就是我覺得我需要立刻改變我打扮方式的時候。

Matt
麥特

I immediately felt like I needed to change the way I dressed when I arrived in Peru. I'd been very blessed to travel all summer long, following the eternal sunshine. However, on the south hemisphere, it was winter! I had to get my alpaca coat right away.

我一到秘魯就馬上覺得到我要立刻改變我的穿著。我整個夏天都很幸運可以在無止盡的陽光下旅行。但是在南半球的時候，就變成冬天了！我那時候必須要立刻去買駝馬的大衣。

Becca
貝卡

When I was traveling in Honduras, I dressed the way I would dress every day here in the U.S.A white tank top and a pair of shorts. However, I started to see guys looked at me in a very weird way. They checked my whole body out unapologetically. I quickly looked around me and found out that no tourists were dressed like me. I quickly went back to

服裝和傳統服飾

the hotel and changed to less revealing dress.

當我在洪都拉斯的時候，我就穿我平常在美國穿得這樣。一件白色背心跟短褲。但是我突然開始發現那裡的男人用很奇怪的眼光看我。他們是一點也不抱歉的看我全身。我立刻看看周遭的人然後發現那裡的觀光客沒有穿得像我這樣。所以我立刻回飯店換一些比較沒有那麼露的衣服。

03 Question
In your opinion, what is the best-dressed city?
對你來說，哪一個城市的人最會穿衣服？

Michelle
蜜雪兒

I think people in Paris can dress the best. They dress up even when they dress down! It's amazing to see how effortless it is for them to show their styles. And not just women, men, too are really good at dressing up as well. I'm very impressed with the high percentage of people that can dress well in that city!

我覺得巴黎的人最會穿衣服。他們就算沒打扮也像有打扮。看到他們那麼不費力跟輕鬆的展現出他們的風格真的很厲害。而且還不只是女人而已，男人也是很會打扮。我對於他們那裡的人那麼高比例的會穿衣服感到很震撼。

I think people in Hawaii know how to dress the best! Did you know that Aloha shirts are considered formal wears there? Most of their outfits are no more than bikinis, swimming shorts, beachwear, and flip-flops. The most important part is that it is okay to dress like that, too!

我覺得在夏威夷的人最會穿衣服！你知道夏威夷花襯衫在這裡是正式的穿著嗎？他們大多數的服裝就是比基尼、泳褲、海灘服飾還有夾腳拖鞋。最重要的是他們這樣穿也是可以被接受的！

I think Korean people have a very distinct style, and I

find it very cool. They are usually very confident and they have very different styles from the rest of the world. The colors in their outfits are very bold and so as the styles. They are not afraid to show themselves in my opinion!

我覺得韓國人有很獨特的穿衣風格而且我覺得很酷。他們通常都很有自信，而且他們的風格跟其他地方的人也很不一樣。他們服裝的用色都很大膽而且他們的風格也是。我覺得他們真的很不怕展現他們自己。

Useful expressions

▲ people watching 觀察周遭的人

❶ My favorite thing to do is just people watching and drink a cup of coffee on a Sunday morning.

我最喜歡做的事就是在禮拜天觀察周遭的人並且喝杯咖啡。

▲ get the hang of it 抓到訣竅

❷ It'll get easier once you get the hang of it.

等你抓到訣竅之後就會越來越簡單了。

▲ get a sense of 體驗一下當…的感覺，感覺一下…

❸ Try to play around with the hammock, so you can get a sense of how it works. It will help when we start the aerial yoga later.

試著玩一玩那個吊床，所以你可以感覺一下它是怎麼運作的。這對我們等下開始做空中瑜珈很有幫助。

⚓ talent show 才藝表演

❹ The kids are taking turns doing the talent show on stage.

孩子們都在台上輪流表演才藝。

⚓ rock 把⋯做得很好，把⋯穿得很好看

❺ She is going to rock the presentation! She's been practicing all week!

她的簡報一定會做得很好的！她整個禮拜都在練習。

⚓ mix and match 混搭

❻ These bikinis are buy one get one free, and you can mix and match the tops and the bottoms.

這些比基尼都是買一送一，而且你上下身還可以混搭。

⚓ go back in time 時光倒流，回到過去

❼ If I could go back in time, I would tell my parents that I loved them very much.

如果時光可以倒流的話，我想要跟我的爸媽說我很愛他們。

⚓ makeover 改裝

❽ She always does a big makeover when she ends a relationship.

她每次結束了一段戀情就會做一個大改造。

19 Specialty Food
美味名產

Unit

 背景起源

Going through your pictures and choosing a favorite food from your trip is never an easy chore. We all have had some truly sensational meals in some once-in-a-life time restaurants and in some distant locations. We learned how to say "delicious" in every possible language from those truly blessed moments. However, sometimes it's the simple dishes that have been executed in the most authentic way stand out; a bowl of Pho by the street in Vietnam or a slice of Margarita pizza in Italy for instance. To add on an exotic note, it only exists in those places. The specialty food we tasted not only brought us a happy belly, but also stories and great memories about the place. Have you found foods that are worth traveling for yet? Don't worry, they don't run out. You still have the whole world to explore.

要從旅行的照片裡面翻出最喜歡的一道食物從來就不容易。我們都有過在某個遙遠的地方，然後某個一輩子難得去一次的餐廳吃到令我們驚為天人的美食。因為那些幸運的時刻，我們學會了怎麼用各種可能的語言說「好好吃！」但是我們最喜歡的通常都是那些很簡單但是卻很道地的食物。例如在越南路邊吃到一碗牛肉河粉，或是一片在義大利吃到的瑪格麗特披薩。而且那些都只有在當地才吃的到，因為這樣，那些食物又更有異國風情一些。這些美食不只讓我們吃得開心，也讓我們得知一些關於這個地方的故事並留下關於這個地方美好的回憶。你找到你願意旅行去吃的一道菜了嗎？別擔心，他們永遠都吃不完！而且你還有一整個世界可以探索！

Dialogue 情境對話　MP3 37

Mia and her local friend Leilani are going to a local health bar for Acai Bowl in Hawaii.
蜜雅和她當地的好朋友蕾拉妮要去夏威夷當地一間健康飲食店買 Acai Bowl（巴西莓果冰沙）。

Leilani: I'm gonna take you to try one of the things I love in the world.	蕾拉妮：我要帶你去吃一個我全世界最喜歡吃的東西之一。
Mia: I'm excited. What is it? We're going surfing later. I don't want to be too stuffed.	蜜雅：我好期待喔！我們要吃什麼啊？我們等下要去衝浪耶。我不想要吃太飽。

Leilani: It's called "Acai Bowl". It's a smoothie made from Acai berries, which has a lot of natural antioxidants, and on top of the smoothie, they put fresh blueberries, strawberries, bananas, granola and honey. It's actually pretty filling, but doesn't make you feel too stuffed.

蕾拉妮：我們要吃的東西叫做「巴西莓果冰沙」。它是一個用有很多天然抗氧化劑的巴西莓果做成的冰沙，然後在冰沙上面他們會放新鮮的藍莓、草莓、香蕉、穀片，還有蜂蜜。吃完其實會飽，可是不會讓你太飽。

Mia: Wow, that sounds amazing and so healthy at the same time!

蜜雅：哇！聽起來好棒喔，而且同時間又很健康！

Leilani: Yeah, it's very healthy and it's actually pretty perfect to eat this before surfing. It gives you energy and it's relatively light.

蕾拉妮：對啊！超健康而且其實蠻適合在衝浪之前吃的！它會給你能量而且相比之下熱量又不會太高。

Mia: Let's give it a try.

蜜雅：我們快來試試看吧。

(After they get their Acai Bowl)

（在他們拿到他們的巴西莓果冰沙之後）

Leilani: So what do you think?

蕾拉妮：你覺得怎麼樣？

Mia: It's even better than what I expected. They are not stingy giving out all these fresh fruits!

蜜雅：比我想像的還要好吃！他們給新鮮水果都超不小氣的！

Leilani: No way, that's one of the selling points!

蕾拉妮：當然不會啊，那是他們的賣點之一！

Mia: I wish we had this back home, too! Can you make this at home?

蜜雅：我真希望我們家那也有賣這個！你可以在家自己做這個嗎？

Leilani: Yeah, usually we can find the frozen Acai berries at local supermarkets, so we just make them at home sometimes. But of course it's easier to buy one, if you don't crave it every day.

蕾拉妮：可以啊！通常可以在這裡的超市買到冷凍的巴西莓果，所以有時候就可以在家做冰沙。但是如果你不是天天想吃的話，當然直接去買會比較簡單。

美味名產

Mia: I have to look this up. It's perfect to substitute for some unhealthy meals I have.

蜜雅：我要來查一下。我覺得如果用這個來取代我一些不健康的飲食的話會很好！

Leilani: Goodbye McDonald's!　　　　　蕾拉妮：掰掰麥當勞！

　　MP3 38

	If you visited countries where people ate the following foods, would you try any of them: monkeys, snakes, dogs, and insects? Why or why not?
01 Question	如果你到一個會吃猴子、蛇、狗，還有昆蟲的國家旅行，你會吃任何一樣嗎？為什麼會或是為什麼不會？

 Michelle 蜜雪兒

I just threw up a little in my mouth! I would probably sue them about abusing animals or potentially poisoning the visitors. I hope they have very good reasons not because they have great proteins. I'm all acted up just by thinking about it. Anyways, to answer your question, probably not. I mean never. Ever!

我想到就想吐！我應該會告他們虐待動物還是意圖讓他們的遊客中毒。我希望他們吃這些東西的原因不只是因為有豐富的蛋白質。我光用想的就氣起來了。好啦，所以來回答你這題，我應該不會試任何一樣，

我是說，永遠都不會，永遠！

Matt
麥特

I'm intimidated, but I would probably give it a shot. They would probably taste like chicken, right? I mean as long as I'm not doing something illegal. It would be part of their culture after all. I think I would want to experience the country in the most authentic way.

我會怕，可是我覺得我應該會試試看。反正應該都吃起來像雞肉對吧？我的意思是說，反正只要是不違法，這畢竟也是他們文化的一部份。我應該會想要用最道地的方式體驗這個過家。

Becca
貝卡

I think it would be pretty unlikely. I've always been pretty picky about food already. I mean, I don't consider myself a foodie, but I care about what I eat. As far as I'm concerned,

I'm <u>not the biggest fan of</u> monkeys, snakes, dogs, and insects.

我覺得應該是不太可能。我本來就蠻挑食的。我不是說我是美食家，可是我真的很在乎我吃了什麼。我個人是沒有特別喜歡吃猴子、蛇、狗還是昆蟲啦。

02
Question

What is one specialty food you tried and you would want to go back and eat it again?
你有沒有吃過哪一個名產是你想要再回去吃一次的？

 Michelle
蜜雪兒

I tried the prosciutto with cantaloupe in Italy. I was a bit skeptical at the beginning because it was basically raw ham with melon, but when I tried it, it was the perfect marriage of the foods. It's savory and sweet, very juicy and simply divine. This appetizer is definitely the embodiment of "Less is more." I tried it in a couple of restaurants here, but <u>it just wasn't quite the same.</u>

　　我在義大利有吃過帕馬火腿（煙薰過很薄的火腿）和哈密瓜。一開始我很懷疑這個生火腿跟香瓜的組合，可是我一吃就發現這個組合真是太完美了。又鹹又甜，而且非常多汁，反正就是很完美。這個開胃菜真的是實踐「少就是多」。我有在這裡的幾家餐廳點這個，可是就是跟在義大利吃到的那個不太一樣。

Matt
麥特

　　I would definitely go back to Spain for their Paella. It just has everything I love. Seafood, rice, saffron spices, ...etc. I just love it. I even knew I was going to love it when I saw it. The smell was just impossible to resist. And once I tried it, I knew I was <u>hooked</u>. I would definitely go back again and again for that.

　　我一定會回去西班牙吃他們的西班牙海鮮燉飯。那燉飯裡面有我所有喜歡吃的東西。海鮮、飯、番紅花香料等等。我超愛的。我一開始光看到那道菜我就知道我會超愛這道菜的。那道菜的味道是無法抵擋的。而且我一吃，我就知道我上癮了。我一定會回去很多次去吃這道菜。

I would want to go back to Australia for their meat pies. I love how the Aussies make their pies savory. There are so many great restaurants that specialized in making meat pies as well, so imagine the competition. You gotta be good enough to sell your meat pie! I always check on the reviews on YELP before I go in any restaurants. Therefore, so far my experiences with meat pies are still really satisfactory.

我會想要回澳洲吃他們的肉派。我很喜歡澳洲人把他們的派做成鹹的！而且那裡也有很多餐廳是專賣肉派的，所以你可以想像那裡的競爭。你一定要夠厲害才可以賣你的肉派！而且我去任何餐廳前都會先用 yelp 查一下評價，所以目前為止我在那吃過的肉派都很令我滿意！

03
Question

What is the scariest thing you tried? How was it?
你吃過最恐怖的是什麼？吃起來怎麼樣？

Michelle
蜜雪兒

Puffer fish sashimi in Japan was the scariest thing I've ever tried. I can literally say that I risked my life trying this dish. Sweat was coming out from my palms when I knew that there was still a very small chance for me to get seriously poisoned eating this dish. Normally, I wouldn't do that, but I just really wanted to challenge myself on this one. So that I can tell you that I've tried it. It wasn't too cheap, but the meat tasted really pure and clean. It was a good dining experience, but it was not worth risking my life. Nevertheless, I'm still glad to say that I've tried it.

我在日本吃的河豚生魚片是至今我吃過最恐怖的東西。我真的可以說我是冒著生命危險吃了這道菜。當我知道還是有很小的機會會嚴重中毒的時候，我的掌心都在冒汗。正常來說我不會想要吃，可是我真的很想挑戰，所以現在我可以跟你說我試過了。它其實沒有很便宜，但是那個肉質真的很純淨和乾淨。那是一個還不錯的美食體驗，可是我是覺得不值得我冒生命危險啦！不過我還是很高興我試過了。

美味名產

Matt
麥特

Have you heard of "balut" before? It's the developing duck embryo people eat in Southeast Asia. Yep, it's a boiled egg with actual developing duckling inside. The first time I saw it by the street in Vietnam, I thought they just accidentally picked the wrong egg! Little did I know that they chose the ones with the ducklings inside on purpose! I had to try it just for the sake of it. I am still a little freaked out till now. It was scary, but supposedly they are really nutritious and restorative food for women that are pregnant.

你有聽過「鴨仔蛋」嗎？它就是東南亞人會吃的正在發育中的鴨胚胎蛋。對的，就是水煮蛋裡面有一隻正在發育中的真的小鴨子。我第一次在越南的路邊看到的時候還以為他們是不小心選錯蛋了，結果後來才知道他們就是故意要選裡面有小鴨子的！就是看在這麼奇怪的份上，我當時一定要吃一下。我現在還是有點嚇壞了。真的很恐怖，但是據說對懷孕的人是很有營養也是對修復身體很好的。

Becca
貝卡

The scariest thing I have ever tried was the stinky Tofu in Taiwan. It is notorious for its stickiness, but the crazy part is that the stinkier it is, the better it is according to the locals. The reason why it is stinky is because it's basically fermented Tofu. Gross, I know, but the locals deep-fried the tofu and served it with Kim chi. I gotta say that it did not taste as scary as it smelled and that I'm glad I gave it a try.

我吃過最恐怖的是台灣的臭豆腐！它就是以它的臭惡名昭彰！但是奇怪的是當地人說他是越臭越好吃。會這麼臭的原因是因為它是發酵過後的豆腐。很噁心我知道，但是當地人油炸豆腐，然後再放泡菜在上面。我必須說其實它吃起來沒有聞起來那麼可怕，而且我很高興我有試試看。

美味名產

 Useful expressions

⚓ **...is never an easy chore** …從來就不是一件簡單的差事。

❶ Planning for a family reunion is never an easy chore, especially when you have a big family.

計劃家庭聚會從來就不是一件簡單的差事，尤其當你有很多家人的時候。

⛵ **give it a try** 試試看

❷ I don't know how well I will do, but I want to give it a try.

我不知道我可以做得多好，可是我想要試試看。

⛵ **I just threw up in my mouth a little.** 剛剛在我嘴裡吐了一點；⋯讓我想吐

❸ She is so fake that I just threw up a little in my mouth.

她實在是假到讓我想吐了。

⛵ **foodie** 美食家

❹ You know she is a foodie when she waits in line for 3 hours just for an appetizer.

當她可以為了一個開胃菜排隊三個小時，你就知道她是個美食家。

⛵ **not the biggest fan of...** 沒有特別喜歡⋯

❺ I'm not the biggest fan of politics, so I was really bored when they were talking about politics.

我沒有特別喜歡政治，所以當他們在聊政治的時候，我覺得很無聊。

⛵ **It's just not quite the same.** 感覺就是不太一樣

❻ It's just not quite the same when he is not here.

他不在的時候，感覺就是不太一樣。

⚓ hooked 上癮

❼ He is really hooked on the on-line games.

他真的對線上遊戲很上癮。

⚓ just for the sake of... 看在⋯的份上

❽ You should at least give it a shot just for the sake of your team.

看在你的團隊的份上，你至少要試一試。

Wine
美酒

20

Unit

 背景起源

Going wine tasting in your vacation is like the <u>icing on the cake</u>. It makes the whole trip that much better. Besides, sometimes you get to try wines that can only be found in those specific regions. I often find myself being introduced to wines like they are people. This is Chardonnay and that is Merlot. Very nice to meet you guys. They each have their own personalities, appearances and their own friends. This one goes very well with chicken and that one <u>pairs</u> perfectly <u>with</u> chocolate. It is indeed a sensory experiment and examination. Among all the glasses of wine you taste, there are going to be a few of them you find yourself in love with, and if you have enough budget, you can bring them home with you. They will surely be good souvenirs from your trip! Cheers!

在你的假期中去品酒就像在蛋糕上面放上糖霜一樣，讓整個旅程更加的美好。除此之外，你有的時候還可以試喝只有在那個地區才有出產的酒。我常常發現當別人在跟我介紹酒的時候，好像在介紹人一樣。這是夏多內，那是梅洛。很高興認識你們。他們都有自己的個性和外表，也有自己的朋友。這瓶和雞肉很搭，那瓶跟巧克力是絕配！品酒真的是感官的實驗也是檢驗。在這麼多杯酒之中，你可能會愛上其中幾個，而如果這時候你也還有足夠的預算的話，你還可以帶它們回家。而那也會是很棒的紀念品呢！乾杯！

 Dialogue 情境對話 *MP3 39*

Caroline and Brandon are doing <u>wine tasting</u> at Napa Valley.
凱若林和布蘭登正在納帕品酒。

Caroline: Yay, we made it! Aren't you glad that we made a reservation now? This place is <u>packed</u>!	凱若林：耶！我們終於到了！你現在有沒有很高興我們有先預約？這裡超多人的！
Brandon: Yes, I am indeed. Thanks again for planning this for us Caroline.	布蘭登：有啦！我真的很高興我們有先預約。再次謝謝你幫我們安排這個行程啊凱若林。
Caroline: No problem. I also did a little bit research on their wine here.	凱若林：沒什麼啦！我也有查了一下這裡的

There are a lot of wines to try in this winery, so I think our game plan should be picking different wines and then we can try many different ones.

酒。這個酒莊有超多酒可以試的，所以我覺得我們的戰術應該是要挑不一樣的酒試喝，然後我們就可以喝到很多不一樣的了。

Brandon: Yes, your honor. No objections to that!

布蘭登：好的庭上。我沒有異議。

(They started wine tasting)

（他們開始品酒）

Caroline: How do you like yours?

凱若林：你喜歡你的嗎？

Brandon: I like the nutty finish on this Sauvignon Blanc. It's really perfect for a hot day like this. How's yours?

布蘭登：我喜歡這白蘇維濃最後有堅果香的結尾。在像今天那麼熱的天氣，喝這真是太棒了。

Caroline: My Cabernet Sauvignon is really smooth. I can totally see this one pair well with steak. Yum! Should we get a bottle of this? We'll enjoy it.

凱若林：我的卡本內蘇維濃真的很順。我覺得拿這個搭牛排一定很搭。好吃耶！我們要不要買一瓶？我們一定會很喜歡。

Brandon: Is that your favorite out of all though? I kind of like the Chardonnay at the beginning the best.

布蘭登：可是那是你裡面最喜歡的一瓶嗎？我好像最喜歡一開始的那瓶夏多內。

Caroline: I like that one, too, but it's a bit too dry for me I think.

凱若林：我也喜歡那瓶，可是我覺得對我來說有點太不甜了。

Brandon: Alright then, let's get a bottle of the Cabernet Sauvignon. Let's bag a little San Francisco home.

布蘭登：好吧！那我們就買一瓶卡本內蘇維濃吧！打包一點舊金山回家！

 三問三答　　MP3 40

01
Question

Do you sign up for wine tasting tours when you have a chance? Why? Why not?
你通常有機會的話都會報名品酒的行程嗎？為什麼？為什麼不會？

美酒

243

Of course. <u>What is vacation without wine</u>? You will be amazed at how many fine wineries there are in the world. And sometimes, you will get to try some of the most unique wines when you are traveling. I always look for wine tasting tours and often end up taking lots of wine back home to add on to my wine collection at home.

當然會啊！度假沒有酒算什麼度假呢？你會很驚訝世界上有多少好的酒莊。而且通常在你旅行的時候，你可以嚐試到很多獨特的酒。我都一直在找品酒的行程，而且通常在品酒之後，我都會買很多酒回家加入我的收藏。

I don't look for it particularly, but if it is a popular thing to do there, then I would definitely want to try it out. I used to volunteer at several wineries around the world, and it was definitely one of my most valued memories. I learned a lot and had a lot of fun doing it. <u>There's a lot to it</u> than how I imagined it.

我不會特別找品酒的行程，但是如果那是當地很受歡迎的行程的話，那我就一定想要嘗試一下。我之前有在世界各地很多酒莊打工換宿，那個回憶一定是我最珍惜的之一。我學到了很多而且在打工的過程也玩得很開心。製酒比我想像的還要繁複許多。

Becca
貝卡

Naturally, I would love to, but I usually go to websites like Groupon or LivingSocial to look for good deals. It is usually not much to do wine tasting. However, I found deals that not only include wine tasting, but you also get a free bottle of wine at the end of the wine tasting or you get some discounts. They are pretty decent wines, too!

我當然想，可是我通常也都會上一些網站像是酷朋或是團購網站 LivingSocial 找一些便宜的。通常品酒是不會很貴啦，可是我都找得到很多是包含品酒，然後你品酒之後還可以拿走一瓶免費的酒，或是有些折扣買酒。而且他們也是蠻好的酒喔！

美酒

Can you use one adjective to describe your last wine-tasting experience?

你可以用一個形容詞來描述你上一次品酒的經驗嗎?

Michelle
蜜雪兒

"Scrumptious!" I went to the Volcano Winery in big Island. They have the most exotic wines I have ever tried, and they were just insanely scrumptious! They have local fruit wines and honey wines that are 100% made from the island's macadamia nut trees. It was a truly sensational wine tasting experience. Who would have thought wines can be so tasty!

「超級美味!」我上次去了大島的火山酒莊。他們有我喝過最異國風的酒,而且他們超級美味的!他們有當地的水果酒,也有是百分之百用島上的夏威夷果樹做成的蜂蜜酒。那真的是讓我很震撼的品酒經驗。誰知道酒也可以這麼美味!

Matt
麥特

My last wine tasting experience was very "friendly". I was working at a winery at Mendoza in Argentina the last time I went wine tasting. I had a day off, and I was doing the wine tasting at the place I worked. I met a bunch of travelers from all over the world. We started to chat, and we actually bought a few bottle of wines and enjoyed them together afterwards. I'm going to visit one of them next week.

我上次去品酒的經驗是很「友善的」。我上次品酒的時候是我在阿根廷門多薩的一間酒莊工作的時候。我那天休假，然後就在那裡品酒。我認識了一群從世界各地來的旅行者，我們大家都開始聊天，然後後來我們還買了幾瓶酒一起享用。我下禮拜就要去拜訪他們其中一個。

Becca
貝卡

"Tipsy" would be the best adjective to describe my last wine tasting experience. The last time I went wine tasting, I was at Hunter Valley at Sydney. I went with an empty

stomach because I was running late for the tour. It was a very beautiful place and their famous Semillon there was just heavenly. I got tipsy very fast with both the wine and the view. It was overall a very pleasurable experience.

「微醺」可能是最好的形容詞來形容我上次品酒的經驗。我上次去品酒的時候我是去雪梨的獵人谷。因為我差點就趕不上這個品酒的行程，所以我是空腹去的。那裡超美的，而且他們有名的榭密雍白葡萄酒真是太美好了。我很快就因為美酒和美景微醺了。整體來說那真是很開心的經驗。

03 Question

What is the one word anyone should know before they go wine-tasting?
你覺得每個人去品酒前都要知道的一個字是什麼？

Michelle
蜜雪兒

I think everyone should know the word "complex" before they go wine tasting. People that are really into wine can be very judgmental sometimes. When I first started doing wine tasting, the word "complex" was always my go-to word. If I was not too sure about the wine, I would say: "it's very complex", and I could usually pass test easily.

　　我覺得每個人在去品酒之前都應該要知道「口感複雜的」這個字。那些對酒很瞭解的人有的時候還蠻愛評斷其他人的。我一開始品酒的時候，「口感複雜的」這個字一直是我的仰賴的字眼。如果我對於喝的酒不太確定的話，我就會說"這酒的口感複雜"，然後就會輕易通過考驗。

Matt
麥特

　　When I first started going wine tasting, I was in the dark. I think the most challenging part was to pronounce the wine I like.　Of course it is okay to explore a little bit at the beginning, but once you find the wine you actually like, try to look it up and pronounce the name of the bottle correctly.　I can tell you my favorite wine is Pinot Noir.　What is yours?

　　我一開始品酒的時候，我毫無頭緒。我覺得最難的部分就是念出我喜歡的酒的名字。當然囉，在一開始的時候可以探索一下自己喜歡什麼樣的酒，但是一旦你找到你喜歡的酒，試著查一下正確的發音。我可以跟你說我最喜歡的酒是 Pinot Noir（黑皮諾）。那你最喜歡的酒是什麼呢？

美酒

Becca
貝卡

"Dry" is the word I think people should know because that's usually how people ask you about wine. "Do you like dry wine or sweet wine?" Dry is a wine vocabulary, which means it's not sweet and it is less smooth.

我覺得大家應該要知道「干（不甜）」這個字因為通常大家都會問你這個。「你喜歡干（不甜）酒還是甜酒？」干飾品酒的單字，也就是不甜或是比較不順的意思。

 Useful expressions

⚓ **icing on the cake** 好上加好；錦上添花

❶ Not only did he get accepted to the school, he also got the scholarship. What an icing on the cake!

他不止被這所學校錄取，而且他還拿到獎學金。真的是錦上添花耶！

⚓ **pair with** 配對

❷ It is very important pair the right wine with your food. The right wine will make the food taste better.

幫你的食物配對的酒是很重要的。對的酒會讓你的食物吃起來更好吃。

⛵ wine tasting 品酒

❸ Make sure you don't wear white clothes when you go wine tasting.

你去品酒的時候記得不要穿白色的衣物喔！

⛵ packed 很擁擠的；充滿…的

❹ Disneyland is always packed with kids.

迪士尼樂園永遠都是充滿著小孩的。

⛵ What is X without Y? 沒有 Y 的 X 算什麼 X？

❺ What is home without love?

沒有愛的家算什麼家？

⛵ there's a lot to it 這之中學問很多

❻ Surfing is not as easy as what it looks. There's a lot to it.

衝浪沒有看起來那麼簡單。這之中學問很多。

⛵ go-to 仰賴的…

❼ He is always my go-to guy whenever I have IT issues.

每次我有科技的問題的話，我就會去找他。

美酒

21 Shopping
購物

Unit

 背景起源

Some travelers get to know a place through its historical museums and monuments, while others through its scenic landscapes or traditional cuisine, but for globetrotters who love to shop, there are no truer ways to experience a place than by bargaining with merchants in a bazaar, browsing the handcrafts of local artisans or trying on designer clothes at the boutique in town. Shopping in a foreign country can be both exciting and rewarding, but it's not without its downfalls. The art of bargaining is often a challenge for visitors that are used to <u>fixed prices</u> at their mall at home, and the sea of cheap <u>knock-offs</u> and tacky souvenirs in just about any major tourist destination makes it difficult to tell when you've found a true local gem. So do your homework and happy treasure hunting!

有一些遊客喜歡從具歷史性的博物館或是紀念碑來認識一個地方，

其他人則是從美麗的風景或是傳統的美食切入。但是對於熱愛購物的世界旅行者來說，沒有什麼比在市集裡跟店家殺價，在當地的工匠店裡瀏覽手工藝品，或是在鎮上的精品店裡試穿設計師服飾更直接認識這個地方的辦法。在國外購物可以是很刺激也很值回票價的，但是它還是有它的缺點。對於在自己國家時習慣於固定價格的遊客們來說，殺價是很具挑戰性的。在每個觀光景點都有賣的眾多便宜的盜版，和廉價的紀念品之中，很難說你是不是真的找到了當地的好貨。所以行前一定要做好功課，祝你尋寶成功！

 **Dialogue 情境對話** MP3 41

Cecilia and Gracie are shopping around at Queen Victoria Building in Sydney.
蓆席利雅和葛雷絲正在雪梨的維多利亞購物中心逛街。

Cecilia: Wow Gracie, I feel like I went back in time at this mall. This is such a quaint place.	蓆席利雅：哇葛雷絲，我覺得在這個購物中心裡我好像時光倒流回到從前。這真是一個古色古香的地方。
Gracie: Yeah, you're right. This place was built in 1890 as a big marketplace, but they kept this historical building and changed it into	葛雷絲：對啊，你說的沒錯。這個地方是在 1890 年建造的市集，但是現在他們保留下來

購物

a fancy shopping center now.

這個歷史建築，然後把它改造成一個高級的購物中心。

Cecilia: There is some amazing marketing strategy going on here. A historical building combining with modern boutiques. Impressive.

蔗席利雅：這背後有用了很厲害的行銷策略。歷史建築跟現代精品店，真不錯。

Grace: Haha...Dear marketing manager, you're on vacation now. Chill, and let's do some shopping!

葛雷絲：哈哈…親愛的行銷經理，你現在在放假。放輕鬆，我們來逛街啦！

Cecilia: Oops, sorry I couldn't help it. That's what happens when you are in the office twenty-four seven brainstorming marketing strategies.

蔗席利雅：啊呀，不好意思我不是故意的。這就是你二十四小時都在公司裡想著行銷策略的結果。

Grace: It's okay. I was just picking on you. Although I have to say that the prices here are all on the higher end, so I can take you somewhere else if you are looking for some cheap buys.

葛雷絲：沒關係啦，我只是在挑你毛病。不過這裡的價格都比較高喔，如果你只是想要找一些比較便宜的東西我也可以帶你去別的地方。

Cecilia: Yeah, it's cool. I don't mind window-shopping. This building is so stunning. Look at the stained glass window and the staircase.

蔫席利雅：好啊，沒關係。我也很喜歡看看就好。這棟建築物真的好美。你看那個彩色玻璃，還有樓梯。

Gracie: And I love the historical clock there. Did you see that?

葛雷絲：還有我喜歡他們的歷史時鐘。你有看到嗎？

Cecilia: Let's take some pictures of this place. I think I might have some ideas about how we can develop our historical buildings back home.

蔫席利雅：我們來照點相好了。我有一個很好的點子可以開發我們的歷史建築物。

Gracie: Are you serious? What happens to goodbye work, and hello vacation?

葛雷絲：你是認真的嗎？不是說好掰掰工作，哈囉渡假？

Cecilia: You're right, I'm sorry. Let's go grab a cocktail somewhere.

蔫席利雅：你說的對。對不起，好那我們去哪裡喝杯調酒好了。

購物

255

三問三答  MP3 42

01 Question

Are you a mall person? Why? Why not?
你是一個喜歡購物中心的人嗎？為什麼？或為什麼不是？

Michelle
蜜雪兒

Am I a mall person? Excuse me, I can live in a mall. Of course, I am a mall person, and I'm not shameful about it at all. I love everything about shopping in a mall. You get your nails done, you take home beautiful clothes, and you can sit down at the food court to eat or get a cup of gourmet coffee. There is just so much to see and try on. It is a stress-relief process for me really. Don't you just want to get out and shop a little when you are having a bad day? It just makes everything better.

我喜歡購物中心嗎？不好意思，我還可以住在購物中心裡。我當然喜歡購物囉，而且我一點也不害羞。我喜歡購物的每件事。你可以做指甲，帶漂亮的衣服回家，你還可以在美食街吃東西或喝杯高級的咖啡。在購物中心裡有好多東西可以看跟試穿。對我來說其實真的是一個抒壓的方式。你在心情不好的時候不會想要去買點東西嗎？購物讓每件事情都變得很美好。

Matt
麥特

No, not even a tiny bit. I guess I just don't find material things attractive. Nevertheless, I do have a thing for sporting goods. I guess I don't like shopping, but I do need to get necessities. Yep, that's what I'm trying to say.

一點都不是。物質的東西就真的是一點都不吸引我。不過啦，運動用品店對我來說是我的死穴。我想可能是因為我不喜歡購物，但是我還是得買一些必需品啦。嗯，沒錯，我的意思就是那樣。

Becca
貝卡

Sometimes. I am when there are sales. I don't mind digging out all the goodies even if it means it'll take hours. It's the result that counts. I often find goods that are way

under their original prices. It's amazing how much discount you can get sometimes. Who buys with the original prices nowadays?

　　有的時候是，他們特價的時候我就是。我不介意挖好貨甚至是好幾個小時也沒關係。結果最重要。我常找到很多比原價便宜超多的東西。有的時候看到你拿到多少折扣也是蠻驚人的。現在哪有人用原價買東西啊？

Do you have a killer line for bargaining?
你殺價有哪一句殺手鐧嗎？

Michelle
蜜雪兒

　　I would never bargain. How can you possibly bargain in a mall? It's so not classy. I don't care about one or two more dollars really, and it's just awkward begging for a lower price. I don't know how people can do it. A cold sweat just broke out on my forehead thinking about it. No way José.

我一定不會殺價的。你怎麼可能會在購物中心裡殺價？一點都不優雅。我真的不在意多了一塊還是兩塊，真的，而且要拜託他們壓低價格就是一件蠻尷尬的事。我不懂怎麼有人可以做到。我光想我的額頭就開始冒冷汗了。絕對不可能的啦！

I don't really have one, but I am mostly just honest about it. I'll say something like "It's a little out of my budget, but I would love to get this from you. Do you think we can work something out here?" And it works really well sometimes. Just be sincere I guess. If they like you, they'll give you a good price. But the key is they have to like you.

我沒有什麼殺手鐧耶，不過我通常就是很誠實。我會說：「這個有點超出我的預算，但是我真的很想跟你買。你有什麼好的辦法嗎？」這樣說有的時候真的很有用。我想就是要很誠懇吧。如果他們喜歡你的話，就會給你一個好價錢。不過重點是他們要喜歡你。

I'll say something like if it's xxx dollars, then I'll get it. Of course you can't go crazy low. I always shop around and compare the prices first, and then give a reasonable price. If you do your homework, you usually get what you want with the price you like even more! Although sometimes I'll say it's my birthday...

我會說「如果是×××元的話,我就買了!」不過當然你不能殺太低。我通常都是先到處逛逛然後比較價錢,最後再給了一個合理的價格。如果你有做好功課的話,你通常會買到你喜歡的東西,而且是用你更喜歡的價錢買到的。不過有的時候我會說今天是我的生日⋯

03 **What do you usually shop for when you are traveling?**
Question
你旅行的時候通常想要逛街買什麼?

I like to get things that are made from that place. It just brings back the memories when I see the things I get from those places...Alright...and it's easier for me to remember where I went. It's the true purpose of a souvenir! And I also feel like I can blend in when I'm wearing the stuffs that are made by the local designers there.

我喜歡買是從那個地方製造的東西。當我看到那些東西就會帶我回到在那裡時的回憶…好啦,而且對我來說也比較容易記得我去了哪裡。那就是紀念品真正的意義啊!而且在那裡的時候穿當地設計師做的東西也讓我覺得我比較融入當地!

Like I said, I don't really shop that much at all. However, I like to collect the travel destination magnets when I'm traveling. I always look for a cool one when I'm traveling. I've already had an awesome collection at home. I think I'll

購物

need to get a bigger refrigerator next. Hahaha...

就像我剛剛說的，我真的不太喜歡買東西。但是，因為我旅行的時候喜歡收集旅遊景點的磁鐵。我每次旅行的時候都在找一些酷的磁鐵。我在家裡已經有一些很棒的收集。我想我下個要買的東西應該就是一個大一點的冰箱了！哈哈哈…

Becca
貝卡

I usually shop for local goods that aren't too expensive. I need to get some souvenirs for my boss and coworkers. It's just a nice gesture you know. Foods are usually great to get, or anything that's not too heavy and doesn't take too much room in my luggage really. Handcrafted wares are perfect for example.

我通常喜歡買一些當地的產品，但又不會太貴。因為我通常需要買一些紀念品給我的老闆還有同事。這是一個蠻好表示好意的舉動。食物通常都不錯，或是任何不會太重或是佔我的行李太多空間的東西。例如手工藝品就是很棒的選擇！

Useful expressions

⚠ **fixed price** 定價

❶ I wish I could give you a cheaper price, but everything here has a fixed price.

我也希望我可以給你一個便宜的價錢，可是這裡的東西都是定價的。

⚠ **knock-offs** 盜版商品

❷ That is a horrible knock off of Nike. It says "Nice".

這是一個超爛的 Nike 盜版。上面寫的是 "Nice"。

⚠ **I couldn't help it.** 情不自禁，無法控制

❸ The cupcakes were just too tasty. I couldn't help but eat them all.

那些杯子蛋糕實在是太好吃了。我情不自禁地把它們全部吃掉了。

⚠ **I was just picking on you.** 我剛剛只是在跟你開玩笑啦！我只是故意挑你毛病的啦！

❹ Don't worry! I'm not mad. I was just picking on you!

別擔心啦！我沒生氣。我剛剛只是在開你玩笑啦！

⚠ **Are you a ＿＿＿ person?** 你是喜歡…的人嗎？

❺ Are you a cat person? We have five cats in the house.

你是喜歡貓咪的人嗎？我家有五隻貓喔。

購物

22 Restaurant
餐廳

Unit

 背景起源

Restaurants you encountered during your trip can easily change the whole traveling experience to the better or worse just like that. Before you can react, let's look through your past dining experiences in restaurants when you are on the road. If they are only mediocre, then they don't stand out in your trips at all, but if they are rather great experiences, you talk about it till all of your friends are very jealous. If the experiences are bad though, sometimes we get a little bit dramatic and say something like "I'll never go back!" What is this that we are doing? It seems more than what we think it is. Restaurant reservations to table service, entertainment to engagement—every aspect of the customer experience in a restaurant adds up to the diner's overall satisfaction. We see now, but how do we find good restaurants when we are traveling? If someone came to your hometown, you could tell them exactly where to eat for the best meal at the best prices, using your local knowledge. If only you could tap into this knowledge while traveling. The best way to do this on the road is to follow one specific but very difficult strategy: eat where the locals eat.

　　你在旅行的時候去的餐廳可以很輕易地就改變你整個旅行的體驗。在你反應過來之前，我們來回想看看你過去旅行去過的餐廳好了。如果他們很平庸的話，他們就完全不會出現在你旅行的回憶裡，但是如果是蠻好的經驗，你會一直跟你的朋友說，直到你確定他們都非常的忌妒。如果是不好的經驗的話，我們有的時候會有點誇張然後說了這類的話：「我永遠都不會回去吃了！」我們這樣到底是在幹嘛呢？餐廳的經驗好像比我們想的還要重要一點。從餐廳訂位，到桌邊服務，娛樂到參與，每一個顧客在餐廳的經驗都會影響到顧客整體的體驗。我們現在懂了，可是我們在旅行的時候到底是要怎麼找到好的餐廳呢？如果有人去你的家鄉旅行，你很輕易就可以跟他們說要去哪裡吃最好吃的東西，並且也是最好的價錢，這是運用了你當地人的知識。所以只有在你旅行的時候也有這個知識才可以找到最好的餐廳。旅行的時候最好的辦法很確切，但是也很難：跟著當地人吃就對了！

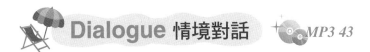

Dialogue 情境對話　♦MP3 43

Terence and his friend Denise are going to a restaurant called Olivier in Utrecht.

泰倫斯和他的朋友德尼絲要去在荷蘭烏特勒支，一家叫做 Olivier 的餐廳。

Terence: This is such a neat restaurant Denise! What is this place?

泰倫斯：這個餐廳好酷喔德尼絲！這裡是哪裡啊？

Denise: Impressive, right? It used to be a church and then they renovated this place to a Belgian pub. They have a good selection of beers and the food is good, too.

德尼絲：很棒對吧？這裡以前是一間教堂，然後他們現在把它改造成一間比利時的酒吧。這裡有很多啤酒的選項，而且食物也很好吃。

Terence: Yeah, it's so spacious, too! They must be doing really good. It's very crowded now.

泰倫斯：對啊，這裡好寬敞喔！他們生意一定很好。現在好多人喔。

Denise: It's always very crowded. I guess that's the only bad thing about this place. You sort of have to yell to talk to each other.

德尼絲：這裡一直都很多人啊！我想這裡唯一不好的地方就是人太多。在這裡講話都要用吼的。

Terence: Nonsense, I think this is fun though. I bet it's really fun to watch any major sports games here.

泰倫斯：胡說，我覺得這樣也很好玩啊！我猜在這看重大賽事一定很好玩。

Denise: You guessed right! It is always fun to watch sports games here. I came here to watch World Cup here and everyone had a blast.

德尼絲：你猜對了！在這裡看球賽真的很好玩。我上次世界盃來這裡看，超好玩的！

Terence: I bet! Look at the old movies that are projected on the wall, too. I just love the ambience here.

泰倫斯：我想也是！你看牆上投影的那些老電影！我好喜歡這裡的氣氛喔！

Denise: Yeah, you're right. I love the dim light and the decoration. It's very cozy to eat here actually.

德尼絲：你說的對。我很愛他們昏暗的燈光跟佈置擺設。在這吃東西很舒適。

Terence: Very cool Denise. You didn't fail my expectations so far in the Netherland. Well done!

泰倫斯：很酷耶德尼絲。目前為止在荷蘭你還沒讓我失望過！做得好！

Denise: Wait till you try their house-brewed beers. I'll take my full compliment then.

德尼絲：等到你喝過他們自己釀的啤酒你在誇獎我！我要全套的誇獎！

Terence: Haha...fair enough. Let's

泰倫斯：哈哈…好啦。

order. I can't wait any longer.

我們來點餐吧。我不能
再等下去了。

三問三答　　MP3 44

01
Question

How do you usually decide which restaurants
you are going to?
你通常都怎麼決定要去哪一間餐廳的？

Michelle
蜜雪兒

There is no reason to eat poorly when you are on
vacation. That's why usually before I go anywhere in the
world, I make sure the meals are great. Restaurant
experience, of course, is a big part of the whole trip.
Besides, asking local tour guides directly, I usually just ask
the front desk of my hotels for recommendations. They
haven't failed me so far. Knock on wood!

　　你在度假的時候實在沒有理由吃很差。這也就是為什麼通常在我決
定要去任何地方之前，我會先確認餐點會是很棒的。在餐廳裡的體驗算
是佔了旅行很大一部分。除了直接問我當地的導遊之外，我也會到飯店

的櫃台請他們幫我推薦。他們目前為止都還沒讓我失望過。老天保佑！

Matt
麥特

I usually just go with the flow and take a chance. You never know whom you are going to meet and what you might get into. That's why I never make any reservation when I'm going to the restaurants. Most of the time, I meet people and they usually have something in mind. Other times, I just go to any restaurant that I think it is interesting. I found many cool little places this way. I might have trouble finding it again, but hey, that's the magical part about it.

我通常就是跟著感覺走耶，然後就冒個險。你永遠不知道你會遇到誰或是會遇到什麼事。這也就是為什麼如果我要去餐廳吃飯的話，我從來都不訂位。大部分的時候，我遇到的人都會有想要去的地方。其他的時候，我就去我覺得蠻有趣的餐廳看看。我都是這樣找到一些很酷的小地方。要我找到去過的餐廳可能有點難，但欸，那也就是它神奇的地方！

Yelp is actually very useful in this case. You will be surprised by how many users it has around the globe. I read the foodie blogger's suggestions and then I Yelp those places. So far, the experiences have been more than satisfactory. I also like to explore APPs, there are a lot of APPs that can tell you where are some good restaurants people like around your location. The bottom line is that if you do your research and you will get the food that's closer to your expectation.

Yelp 在這個時候就很有用耶！你如果知道全球有多少人在用的話你一定會很驚訝。我會先查美食部落客的建議，然後再用 Yelp 查查看那個地方。目前為止我都很滿意啦。我也會用一些 APP，現在有很多 APP 都可以跟你說離你很近的地方大家喜歡的餐廳在哪裡。反正最重要的就是，你一定要做好功課，那你就會吃到跟你預期比較接近的食物啦！

02
Question

In your opinion, what makes a restaurant great?

對你而言,一個好的餐廳要有什麼?

Michelle
蜜雪兒

I think obviously what makes a restaurant great is its food. The quality of the food should be <u>over the top</u> and it speaks for all. All those five stars restaurants work so hard to make sure the quality of the food is great and they always have innovative dishes. One of my <u>pet peeves</u> is to go to a good restaurant and not be able to get good food there. It's just sad.

我覺得很顯然的一個好餐廳一定要有一很好的食物啊!食物的品質應該要很好,那剩下的就沒話說了。所有五星級的飯店都為了食物的品質而努力,而且他們也通常都會有很多創新的菜肴。我的死穴之一就是去一個好餐廳但是卻吃不到好的食物。就只會讓我覺得很悲哀。

Matt
麥特

I think what makes a restaurant great is its fun atmosphere. Eating in a restaurant for me is about the whole dining experience. It's not just the food that I'm going for. I'm going to the restaurant for the music, the fun crowd of people, and if the food happens to be great, too, then awesome. But for me it's not the most important thing.

我覺得一個好的餐廳一定要有很好玩的氣氛。我在餐廳吃飯比較在意的是吃飯整體的經驗。我不是只有為了食物而去的。我去是為了那個餐廳的音樂，好玩的人們，然後如果剛好食物也很好吃的話，那就太棒了。但是對我來說，那並不是最重要的事。

Becca
貝卡

I think what makes the restaurant great is its staff. I think if the restaurant staffs care about their food, it makes such a big difference. The service, the food, the place will be great and it's easy to see if the staff care about their own restaurant, too. If the owner can train their employee right, I think it's not hard to have a great restaurant. Better yet, if they have a reasonable price, too, then it'll be an amazing restaurant.

我覺得一個好餐廳一定要有好的員工。如果餐廳的員工在意他們的食物的話，那就會很不一樣。他們的服務、食物，還有整個地方都會很棒因為他們的員工在意他們自己的餐廳。如果餐廳老闆可以好好的訓練員工的話，我想有個好餐廳應該不是難事。更好的是，如果餐廳價格也很好的話，那就會變成一家超級棒的餐廳。

03
Question
Do you prefer restaurants that are cheap and cheerful or very fancy?
你比較喜歡便宜又歡樂的餐廳還是高級餐廳？

Michelle
蜜雪兒

I prefer restaurants that are fancy. You know how it goes. It's nice to dress up and get all <u>dolled up</u> when you are going to a nice restaurant. Then you don't have to worry about getting food poisoned but just relaxed and enjoy your

dinner. And better yet, if you have a handsome date and then the romantic atmosphere will be very important.

　　我比較喜歡高級餐廳。你知道的。如果要去一間好的餐廳的話，你可以穿得和打扮得很漂亮。然後你也不用擔心會不會食物中毒，可以放鬆的吃飯。更棒的是，如果你有一個很帥的伴的話，那浪漫的氣氛就是很重要的事！

Matt
麥特

　　I prefer the cheap and cheerful restaurants so much more! I was once at this restaurant in Hamburg. It wasn't a fancy restaurant, but the food is really good. My friends and I were just having fun and enjoying ourselves. We didn't realize that we stayed past the restaurant closing time. We apologized, but the owner just shrugged and said he was glad to see us having so much fun at his restaurant. It has become our favorite restaurant ever since then.

　　我比較喜歡去便宜又好玩的地方好多！有一次我在德國漢堡的一間餐廳吃飯。那不是一間很高級的餐廳，但是食物卻非常好吃。我朋友跟我就只是很享受我們的晚餐。我們沒發現我們待到超過關門的時間。我們跟老闆道歉，但他只是聳聳肩跟我們說他很開心看到我們在他的餐廳玩得那麼開心。從那時候開始那裡就是我們最喜歡的餐廳了。

Becca
貝卡

You know, food is food. I don't really feel comfortable spending a lot of money at a restaurant. What I care more is if we are full, and if we have fun! I don't know how some restaurant can feel comfortable charging people so much money for a meal and usually tiny meals as well. I guess I just don't get it.

你知道的，食物就是食物。如果我花很多錢在餐廳的食物上的話，我會覺得不自在。我只在意我們有沒有吃飽，還有有沒有玩得盡興！我不知道為什麼很多餐廳可以為了一餐，自在地跟顧客要那麼多錢。我想我就是不懂這個啦。

⚓ I bet! 我想也是！

❶ She said she's really tired. I bet! She's been working really hard recently.

她跟我說她真的很累。我想也是！她最近真的工作得很辛苦。

⚓ knock on wood 老天保佑（並且敲打木頭來避免惡運發生）

❷ I haven't caught a cold for a year! Oh, knock on wood!

我已經一年沒感冒了。啊！老天保佑！

⚓ go with the flow 隨坡逐流，跟著感覺走

❸ I'm just going to go with the flow and see what happens.

我就只要跟著感覺走，然後看會發生什麼事。

⚓ take a chance 冒點險

❹ Sometimes you need to take a chance in life.

人生有的時候就是要冒點險。

⚓ bottom line 重點是

❺ The bottom line is that everyone is safe. We shouldn't argue anymore.

重點是現在大家都是安全的。我們不應該在繼續吵了。

⚠ **over the top** 標準以上，水準很高

❻ The food here is over the top. I'm sure you will enjoy it.

這裡的食物水準很高。我保證你一定會喜歡的。

⚠ **pet peeves** 死穴

❼ One of his pet peeves is that when someone slams his car door really hard. He gets pretty mad.

他的死穴之一就是如果有人大力的甩他的車門的時候。他會很生氣。

⚠ **dolled up** 打扮得很漂亮

❽ Look at all the girls are all dolled up here. I need to go home and dress up.

你看在這裡的女生都打扮得好漂亮喔。我需要回家打扮一下。

Museum
博物館

背景起源

Museums are places where great collections of art or a certain subject is displayed. It is usually a great place to go if you wish to know more about the subjects. Experts who are the best in those areas collect all the best possible items for you in the museums. We are all very blessed to live in the modern era. We don't have to go through all the fuss to find the bits and pieces. All we have to do is just visit the museums and you see all of them together. Organized and with descriptions on them. What are the better ways to learn things than this? Who says museums are boring? They are the masterpiece of a lot of hard work.

　　博物館是個具有偉大藝術收藏或某個特定主題的展示場所。如果你對某個主題很有興趣的話，通常去博物館是一個很好的選擇。有很多在那些領域是頂尖的專家收集了很多關於那個主題最好的作品，然後存放在博物館裡。我們在這個摩登的時代真的很幸福。因為我們不用大費周章的去找那些零零碎碎的作品。我們只要去一趟博物館，你就可以看到所有的收集了。而且他們還整齊地排列，並且備註介紹。還有什麼比這樣更好的方式學東西呢？誰說博物館很無聊的？它們可是多人辛苦工作的心血結晶。

Dialogue 情境對話 MP3 45

Willy and Alice are working in their study at home.
威力和愛麗絲正在他們家的書房工作。

Willy: I can't believe our summer vacation is coming to an end already! I didn't even do the museum visits like I'm supposed to do.

威力：我不敢相信我們的暑假已經要結束了！我都還沒去我應該要去的博物館。

Alice: What do you have to do? Just visit museums? Can't you just look up the information you need?

愛麗絲：你要去那裡做什麼？只是去參觀博物館嗎？你不能上網查一查需要的資料就好了嗎？

Willy: I'm supposed to be there and choose a few art works that I like and want to analyze. But it's too late. I guess your method will have to do.

威力：我應該要去博物館，選幾個我喜歡的藝術品然後再分析它們。但是太遲了，我想只好用你的辦法了。

Alice: Wait, I have an idea. You can use the Google Virtual Tours in the Google Cultural Institute! I think they offer up to 17 top museums on line.

愛麗絲：等下，我有個點子。你可以用谷歌虛擬導覽去谷歌虛擬博物館啊！我想他們有十七個頂尖的博物館在線上。

Willy: Wait, what do you mean? I can go to the museums now as long as I'm on-line? Is that what you're implying?

威力：等下，什麼意思？你說只要我在線上我就可以去博物館嗎？你是想要說這個嗎？

Alice: That's exactly what I'm hinting genius.

愛麗絲：那就是我想說的天才。

Willy: How though? I mean it sounds great, but how did they do it?

威力：但是怎麼可以？我是說聽起來很棒，可是他們怎麼做到的？

Alice: Simple! They use the Street View technology they do with a Google Map, but then this time they make it into a virtual tour!

愛麗絲：很簡單啊！他們是用谷歌地圖街景的那個技術，但是這次他們把它做成虛擬導覽。

Willy: That's so tight! Have you tried it yet?

威力：超酷的！你有試過了嗎？

Alice: Neh, I just heard it from my art professor.

愛麗絲：還沒，我是聽我藝術課的教授說的。

Willy: Guess who's going to the museum with me?

威力：你猜猜看誰要陪我去博物館啊？

Alice: Oh, Willy, I have my work to do as well! Why don't you help mine once you're done with the museum tour!

愛麗絲：喔威力！我也有作業要做啊！你幹嘛不要導覽完你的博物館之後來幫我。

Willy: Okay, but thanks for the great info! Nice save sis!

威力：好啦，但是謝謝你跟我說這個資訊啊！救得好啊！妹妹！

三問三答　MP3 46

01 Question

What's the best museum you've been to?
你去過最棒的博物館是什麼？

Michelle
蜜雪兒

The best one I've been to is Le Louvre in Paris. The museum itself is an art already, <u>not to mention</u> the famous artworks inside. It took me a while to wait till it was my turn to see Mona Lisa. It's beautiful, but I have to say it was smaller than how I had imagined it. However, I think the best way to store beautiful arts is to store them in a beautiful building. They do it right in Paris!

我去過最棒的博物館是在巴黎的羅浮宮。博物館本身就是一個藝術品了，更別提在裡面那些有名的藝術品。我那時候等了蠻久才換我看蒙娜麗莎的微笑。它真的很美，可是我必須說它比我想像的還要小。但是我想儲存美麗藝術品最好的辦法就是把它們放在漂亮的建築物裡。我想它們在巴黎做得很好！

Matt
麥特

I normally don't go to museums because I think it's a lot of looking around not knowing what they are for me.

However, Bishop Museum in Oahu, Hawaii is a really fun museum. It demonstrates how lava is formed and there are a lot of activities and performances at certain time of the day, such as Hula Dance performance. I didn't get bored at that museum and I took a lot of new knowledge with me home. It was a huge museum, but I was thrilled walking around in it.

博物館

我通常都不喜歡去博物館，因為我覺得通常都是要走來走去，可是都不知道在看什麼。但是在夏威夷歐胡島的主教博物館是一個很好玩的博物館。它展示了岩漿是怎麼形成的，而且那裡不一樣的時間也都有不一樣的表演，例如草裙舞表演。我在那個博物館裡都不覺得無聊，而且也學了很多。那裡超大的，可是我在裡面十分興奮地走來走去！

Becca
貝卡

I thought Uffizi Gallery was an excellence in museums. It was overwhelming to see all the famous works gathered together in one museum. Michelangelo, Da Vinci, Raphael and more. I took my time walking from room to room and trying to absorb the fact that those were the works that I read from history books in class.

我覺得義大利烏非茲博物館是博物館裡面的翹楚。在一個博物館裡面看到那麼多有名的作品其實蠻震撼的。米開朗基羅、達文西、拉斐爾等等。我在每個展示間裡都慢慢地逛然後盡可能地相信在我眼前都是在歷史課本裡面讀到的那些作品。

02 Question

What's the strangest museum you've heard?
你聽過最奇怪的博物館是什麼？

Michelle
蜜雪兒

I heard there's a Museum of Bad Art at Somerville Mass. That's just so <u>out of the box</u>! Normally, we see amazing or beautiful arts in a museum, but in that museum, they look for bad art which has to be original as well. I'm not too sure about the point of the museum yet. Perhaps you can help me?

我有聽說一間在美國薩莫維爾市的糟糕藝術博物館。那真是太有創意了。通常我們都只會在博物館裡看見很棒或是很美的藝術，但是在他們這間博物館，他們要找的是原創就很糟糕的藝術。我現在還是有點不懂他們的用意。或許你可以告訴我？

Matt
麥特

The strangest museum I've heard is the Momofuku Ando Instant Ramen Museumat at Osaka, Japan. The whole museum is decorated with instant noodles, and they also have a section where people can try to make the instant noodles. That is just so bizarre for me.

我聽過最奇怪的是日本大阪的泡麵發明博物館。整間博物館都是由泡麵所佈置而成的，而且他們也有一區是人們可以來試試看怎麼製作泡麵的。對我來說真的超奇怪的。

Becca
貝卡

The Museum of Broken Relationships in Croatia is by far the strangest museum I've heard. What do you do with the stuff that belongs to your past relationships? I put them in a

box or throw them away, but this museum is looking for those remnants of a broken relationship. It's really strange but I'm with them. I think it's so creative.

　　在克羅埃西亞有一間失戀博物館是我目前為止聽過最奇怪的博物館。你失戀之後都怎麼處理那些屬於之前戀情的東西啊？我都把它們放到箱子裡或是丟掉，可是這間博物館都在找那些過去戀情遺留下的的東西。那真的很奇怪，但是我蠻喜歡他們的點子的。好有創意。

03
Question

If you had lots of money to start your own museum, what would you exhibit in it? And what would you call it?
如果你有很多錢可以開你自己的博物館，你會想要展示什麼？你會叫那間博物館什麼呢？

Michelle
蜜雪兒

　　It may be a cliché, but I really want to own a Shoe Museum, and I would name it "In Her Shoes". If I had a lot of money already, I'd like to spend it on shoes. Where do I put all those shoes? How about in a museum? It's the most direct way people can appreciate my great taste in shoes.

聽起來可能很陳腔濫調，可是我真的很想要有我自己的鞋子博物館，而且我會叫它「在她的鞋子裡」如果我已經有很多錢了，我想要花在鞋子上。那我要把鞋子放在哪裡咧？博物館聽起來還不錯吧？那是最直接讓大家看到我對鞋子好品味的辦法。

Matt
麥特

I want to open something extraordinary. It's not a tangible thing, but I think people tend to forget them sometimes. I want to open a "dream" Museum. Dream as in what they want to achieve. I just want to collect many people's dreams and put them together to remind people not to forget them. I would name it: "Museum of the Thing You Call Your Dream".

我想要開一間特別的。那不是具體的東西，可是我們大家常常忘記它。我想要開「夢」的博物館。我是說你想達成的夢想的夢。我想要收集大家的夢想，然後把它們放在一起來提醒大家別忘了他們的夢想。我會叫他：「夢想這個東西博物館」。

Becca
貝卡

If I had a lot of money, I would like to open a Book Museum. There is so much work included to produce a book. A book is an identity, a voice or message the author is trying to tell the world. Everything from the book cover design to the content has been pondered upon thousands of times. The best way is to collect some of the best ones and put them together. It would be called something like "behind the pages".

如果我有很多錢的話我會想要開一間書的博物館。要製造一本書要花好多工夫。一本書是一個身份，一個聲音或是一個作者要傳達給世界的訊息。從封面設計到內容的製作都是被想過好多次的結果。我覺得最好就是搜集很多最好的書，然後把它們放在一起。我可能會叫他「在書的每一頁之後」之類的。

 **Useful expressions**

⚓ **bits and pieces** 零星碎片，零碎的片段

❶ I had no idea what they were talking about. I could only pick up the bits and pieces and tried to guess

UNIT 23・Museum 博物館

what they were talking about.

我真的不知道他們在說什麼。我只能從他們講話的零碎片段來猜他們在說什麼。

⛵ come to an end 結束

❷ All good things come to an end.

天下沒有不散的筵席。

⛵ tight 很酷

❸ I thought the concert was so tight!

我覺得那個演唱會真的超棒的！

⛵ nice save 救得好

❹ Nice save by catching the ball Mitch!

米區！你那球救得真好！

⛵ Not to mention 更別提

❺ I can't believe she always finds time, not to mention the energy, to do her schoolwork.

我不敢相信她還有時間，更別提消耗，來做她學校的作業。

⛵ out of the box 很有創意的，跳出框架思考

❻ He always tells us to think out of the box.

他總是叫我們要跳出框架思考。

Architecture
建築物

Unit **24**

 背景起源

Whenever we travel to places, we are attracted to the famous buildings. It's not that most of us have a deep interest in the architecture or because the travel book tells us it's a must-see. It's more about how the designs of these buildings reflect their time and culture in which they were built. It is perhaps boring to look around the architecture surrounding our everyday lives now. However, imagine what we have now only exists in our time. These buildings would stand tall and tells stories about our everyday lives years later. A lot like photography, architecture captures details of specific moments in time and tells us stories from a long time ago. You want to know what life is like in another country? Guess what is the best way to find out?

每當我們在旅行的時候，我們總是被有名的建築物給吸引。那不是因為我們對建築有濃厚的興趣或是只是因為旅遊書跟我們說那是必去的地方。比較是因為建築設計可以反映當年建造這個建築物的時候，那時的年代和文化。或許現在看看你周遭環境中的建築物好像蠻無聊的。但是想像一下如果這些建築物只有在我們這個年代才存在。這些建築物會高高地站著，告訴好幾年後的人我們每天生活的故事。許多就像攝影、建築物也可以捕捉某個時刻的細節並且跟我們說好久好久以前的故事。你想要知道在別的國家的生活是怎麼樣的嗎？你猜最好的辦法是什麼呢？

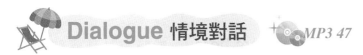

Dialogue 情境對話　MP3 47

Julia and Kate are at the Leaning Tower of Pisa in Italy.
朱麗雅和凱特正在義大利的比薩斜塔。

Julia: We're finally here!!! That's the Leaning Tower of Pisa!

朱麗雅：我們終於到了！那就是比薩斜塔耶！

Kate: The architecture here is gorgeous. Should we take a few selfies with the tower?

凱特：這裡的建築物都好美喔。我們要不要也來跟這個塔自拍一下？

Julia: Hahaha...that man looks like he's pooping the tower. So creative. I'm just gonna pretend I'm pushing it back!

朱麗雅：哈哈哈…那個男的好像在拍他正在把比薩斜塔大出來。好有創意喔。我要來假裝我把它推回去就好了！

Kate: hahaha okay! Got it! Should we go get the tickets to get the tower now?

凱特：哈哈哈好啊！好拍到了！欸我們要不要去買票進去？

Julia: Yeah, what do you think? To go to other buildings is all five euros, but to climb up the Leaning Tower of Pisa costs seventeen euros!

朱麗雅：好啊，你覺得呢？進去其它建築物是五歐元，可是要進去爬比薩斜塔要十七歐元！

Kate: What a rip off! But we are here already. We might as well!

凱特：是想要敲竹槓嗎？那是我們已經在這了。是也可以去一下啦！

Julia: You're right. We've made it this far. Okay, let's go get the tickets then.

朱麗雅：你說的對！我都從這麼遠來了。好吧，我們去買票。

(After they got their tickets)

（在他們買到票之後）

Julia: It feels so weird to climb in a tower that's tilted.

朱麗雅：我覺得在斜塔裡面爬階好奇怪噢。

Kate: And it's spiral stairs here. I'm getting dizzy.

凱特：而且這裡還是旋轉樓梯。我開始暈了。

Julia: Me, too. There are 293 steps in total. We can do this! Come on Kate!

朱麗雅：我也是。總共有兩百九十三階。我們可以的！加油凱特！

Kate: Why did we pay seventeen euros to go through this ordeal?

凱特：我們為什麼要付十七歐元來經歷這災難？

Julia: It will be worth it. Let's take a break and take some pictures!

朱麗雅：會很值得的啦！我們休息一下跟拍些照好了！

Kate: Sounds great to me! I feel like an old lady.

凱特：好啊！我覺得我好像老太婆喔。

Julia: Water, grandma?

朱麗雅：你要喝水嗎，阿嬤？

 三問三答  MP3 48

01 Question

What famous architecture would you like to visit one day?
你有天有想要去哪個有名的建築物嗎？

Michelle
蜜雪兒

I really want to see Taj Mahah in Agra, India one day! It's a mausoleum of a Persian princess that was the favorite wife of the emperor at the time. After she passed away, the emperor was so sad, and decided to build this for her. She still died like a princess. I really want to be there and learn about their love story after all this time. How I wish someone would build a mausoleum for me when I die.

我真的很想要去在印度阿格拉的泰姬馬哈陵！那是一個當時皇帝最喜歡的妻子，一個波斯公主的陵墓。在她去世之後，皇帝就十分的傷心，並且決定要為她打造這個陵墓。她就算死也是很公主的。在過了這麼久以後，我也真的很想要去那裡了解他們的愛情故事。我真希望我死的時候也有人幫我蓋一個陵墓。

Matt
麥特

I really want to visit The Great Pyramids of Giza in Egypt. It's on my ultimate bucket list. I love everything about Pyramids, and there are so many movies with the theme of pyramids. I still cannot believe such structures were built by men. I just want to be there and witness this wonder and mystery.

我真的很想要去埃及的基沙大金字塔。那一直都是在我的終極死前要完成的事的清單中。我很喜歡所有關於金字塔的事，而且也有那麼多部電影都是以金字塔為主題。我還是無法想像這個建築物是人造的。我只想要去那裡目睹這個奇景還有謎。

Becca
貝卡

I haven't had a chance to visit the Great Wall yet, but I really want to visit. They built the wall to keep the enemies from coming in their territory and can you imagine the work they were doing to build the Great Wall? It's 21, 196 km long! And it's from such a long time ago! I really don't know how they made it happen with so little technology back then!

我還沒有機會去過長城，可是我真的很想去。他們當年建造這個墻是為了要避免敵人入侵他們的領土，而且你可以想像他們那時候要花多少功夫嗎？這個長城有兩萬一千一百九十六公里長耶！而且還是從那麼

久以前造的！我實在是不知道他們那時候沒什麼科技，怎麼可以建造出這個！

02
Question

What is the most amazing building you have ever seen?
你看過最棒的建築是什麼？

> Michelle
> 蜜雪兒

The most amazing building I have ever seen is the famous Sagrada Familia built by Gaudi. It's one thing to see it from the picture, but it' another when you see it in person. I thought to myself Gaudi must have lost it. The building is beyond creativity. It's not like anything I've seen before.

　我看過最棒的建築是鼎鼎有名的由高第建造的聖家堂。從照片看是一回事，但是真正看到又是另外一回事。我那時候在想說高第一定瘋了。這個建築物已經超越創意了。我從來沒有看到任何像這樣的建築。

Matt
麥特

By far I have to say Machu Picchu is still the most amazing building I've ever seen, especially with the location, too! It's just amazing to be able to live all the way up in the mountain and so secluded, too. The irrigation system there is pretty cool, too. I wonder if there are more Machu Picchu deeper in the mountain. I wouldn't mind living there at all.

我目前為止是覺得馬丘比丘是我看過最棒的建築，尤其是那個地點！真的很棒他們可以住在深山裡，而且還那麼的隱密。那裡的灌溉系統也很酷。我在想不知道在更深山裡有沒有更多的馬丘比丘。我一點都不介意住在那裡。

Becca
貝卡

I was really impressed with the Lotus Temple in India. The whole building is just extremely peaceful. The shape of the temple is a lotus, and it is all white and you are required to take your shoes off before you enter. They welcome

建築物

people with every religion to come in and pray at the same space. I really feel <u>at peace</u> in that space.

我對印度的蓮花廟印象很深刻。整個建築都十分的平和。它的外型就是一個蓮花,而且它也是全白的。你要進去廟裡之前要把鞋子脫掉。他們歡迎所有宗教信仰在同一個空間一起來禱告。我在那個空間裡真的覺得很安寧。

03 What city's architecture has impressed you the most?
Question
你覺得哪一個城市的建築是最令你印象深刻的?

Michelle
蜜雪兒

Barcelona impressed me the most. Besides the Sagrada Familia, there are Gaudi's works spreading around the city, and I have to say that I'm impressed with them all. It's like your fantasy comes true or your drawing comes alive. He has more imagination and creativity than anyone I know. Many great architecture just dots around the city. I love Barcelona.

巴塞隆納最讓我印象深刻。除了聖家堂之外，高第的作品整個城市裡到處都是。我必須說我真的對他們全部都很印象深刻。那就像是你的幻想成真，或是你的圖畫活了起來。他比我知道的任何人都還要有想像力和創意。有很多的建築到處在城中分佈。我愛巴塞隆納。

Matt
麥特

I am gonna go with Athens. I always have a thing for Greek Mythology. That was my favorite class in college, too. There are so many pantheons in Athens, and it is such an old town. I just find those buildings fascinating and I mean, that was where the Greek God and Goddess lived！！

我選雅典好了！我一直很喜歡希臘神話。那也是我在大學的時候最喜歡的一堂課。在雅典有好多的神殿，而且這個城市也十分的古老。我覺得這整個城市都很吸引人，我是說這是希臘神和女神住的地方耶！

Becca
貝卡

I think the architecture in Istanbul is pretty impressive. There are a lot of magnificent mosques and colorful coffee shops around every corner. The best thing is that usually the best ones are not too far away from each other. I really enjoyed my day walking trips there. It's very exotic and the architecture definitely adds a lot to the city.

我覺得在伊斯坦堡的建築還蠻令人印象深刻的。那裡有很多雄偉的清真寺，附近還有很多色彩繽紛的咖啡店。最棒的是他們最棒的建築都離彼此不遠。我在那裡的時候真的很享受我白天的走路遊覽。非常有異國風味而且那裡的建築真的為那個城市加分了不少。

 **Useful expressions**

⚓ **it's more about** 比較是因為…

❶ I'm not angry because you didn't give me any present. It's more about whether you care or not.

我生氣不是因為你沒給我禮物。比較是因為你在不在乎。

⚓ **rip off** 敲竹槓

❷ You paid 20 dollars for this junk? It's such a rip off!

你用二十元美金買這個破銅爛鐵？那真是敲竹槓。

⚓ **after all this time** 過了這麼久以後，很長的時間之後

❸ They haven't talked to each other after all this time.

都過了這麼久一段時間，他們都還沒有跟對方說話。

⚓ **it's one thing to...but another...** …是一回事，…又是另外一回事.

❹ It's one thing to have a baby, but another to raise one!

有小孩是一回事，但是要養小孩又是另外一回事。

⚓ **lose it** 發火，發瘋

❺ I almost lost it at work today.

我今天上班的時候差點就要發火了。

⚓ **It's not like anything I've...** 這是我從來沒有…過的

❻ I don't know what to do. It's not like anything I've experienced.

我不知道該怎麼辦。這是我從來沒有經歷過的。

⚓ **at peace** 平和，安寧

❼ I always feel at peace after I practice yoga.

我每次做完瑜珈都覺得心情很平和。

Biking
騎自行車

Unit

 背景起源

Touring around a country, a city or just a small town by bike is perhaps the best way to see the place itself with a speed that is fast enough for us to see most of it, but slow enough to enjoy the breeze or meet the people there. On top of that, it's probably a good idea to work out all the extra calories we pick up during a trip. As Ernest Hemingway said it best "It is by riding a bicycle that you learn the contours of a country best, since you have to sweat up the hills and coast down them. Thus, you remember them as they actually are, while in a motor car only a high hill impresses you, and you have no such accurate remembrance of the country you have driven through as you gain by riding a bicycle."

在一個國家、城市或是一個小鎮裡用腳踏車觀光或許是最棒的方式來看這個地方。因為腳踏車的速度夠快，讓我們能看到這裡大部分的地方，但是又夠慢，所以我們可以享受微風或是認識這裡的人們。除此之外，那也是你可以消耗從旅行得到的多餘卡路里的方法。就像海明威說的：「腳踏車是用來瞭解這個國家輪廓最好的辦法因為你要辛苦的爬坡，然後順坡滑下。所以你會記得他們真正是怎麼樣的。而當你坐在車子裡，通常只有很高的山丘會令你印象深刻，但是你並不會像騎腳踏車那樣記得這個你開車過的國家真正是什麼樣子的。」

 Dialogue 情境對話  *MP3 49*

Jay is renting a bike from a bike shop from the clerk Meredith in the Netherlands.

杰正在荷蘭的一家腳踏車店裡跟店員梅若迪絲租腳踏車。

Jay: Hi, so I'm going to take this one for 3 days.

杰：嗨，我要租這台三天。

Meredith: Okay no problem, so just be sure to take it back by noon on the fourth day.

梅若迪絲：好啊，沒問題，所以你就是第四天中午之前帶腳踏車回來就可以了。

Jay: Okay, oh and another thing is that I heard the bike theft here is pretty bad. Do you mind if I pick your brains for any tips of where to park and all that?

杰：好，喔還有就是我聽說這裡腳踏車偷竊案很多。你介不介意我請教你關於要停在哪裡那類的問題？

Meredith: It is bad, but usually if you lock your bike along with all the other bikes, you should be fine. At least you're not the only one on the menu. You know what I mean? However, we do have a policy that if you lost the bike, you have to purchase it.

梅若迪絲：偷竊案是真的蠻多的，但是通常如果你跟著其他的腳踏車停的地方停的話，再鎖好，其實應該還好。至少你不是偷竊案菜單上唯一的一個。你懂我的意思嗎？但是我們有一個政策是如果你遺失了腳踏車，那你就要買它。

Jay: Yes, I understand that. But I would love it if that doesn't happen, so there's really nothing to look out for?

杰：嗯，我知道。但是當然我希望最好是不會發生啦，所以真的沒有什麼是要注意的嗎？

Meredith: <u>For your information</u>, here's the area you want to stay away from (circling on the map) and I can give you an extra lock if that makes you feel better?

梅若迪絲：這裡是你應該要知道的，你應該要遠離這一區（在地圖上圈起）然後我可以給你額外的鎖，如果這樣會讓你放心一點。

Jay: Yeah sure, thanks so much. I would hate it if something bad

杰：好的謝謝你。我也是真的會很難過如果你

happens to your bike, too.

們的腳踏車出了什麼事。

Meredith: You will be fine. Don't worry. So now that's <u>out of the way</u>, let me show you the fun area of this city!

梅若迪絲：不會有事發生的。別擔心。所以現在那個處理好了，讓我來跟你說這個城市哪裡好玩吧！

🧳 三問三答 ✦💿 *MP3 50*

01
Question

Have you been to any <u>bike friendly</u> countries? How was it?
你有去過哪些騎腳踏車很方便的國家嗎？好玩嗎？

Michelle
蜜雪兒

Yes, I was in Copenhagen, Denmark. The city really surprised me with how bike friendly it was. There are bike lanes throughout the city. I never had to share the road with other motor vehicles. I felt pretty safe biking around the city. I'm not the strongest in biking, but I have to say it was

relatively easy to bike around in Copenhagen. I mean I wasn't whining or pouting at all!

　　有啊，我去了丹麥的哥本哈根。我真的還蠻驚訝那個城市竟然騎腳踏車那麼方便。整個城市裡都有自行車道。我從頭到尾都不用跟其他的車擠同一個車道。我那時候覺得在那個城市裡騎自行車是還蠻安全的。我騎腳踏車沒有很強，可是我得說在那城市騎車還蠻容易的。我都沒抱怨還是噘嘴欻。

Matt
麥特

　　Yes, I've been to Amsterdam in the Netherlands. It was really amazing to see the biking population there. It's very common that everyone rides bikes, and rarely do people own cars. The parking lots for the bikes are jaw dropping. It was immense. I literally stood there and wowed for a minute. There are traffic lights for the bikes, bike lanes, all the basics and beyond. I thought it was intriguing to see people all dressed up for work on a bike. They bike with styles for sure.

　　我有去荷蘭的阿姆斯特丹。在那裡騎腳踏車的人口真的很驚人。在那裡大家騎腳踏車是很正常的事，反而比較少人開車。腳踏車的停車場也很令人掉下巴。超大的。我那時候真的是就站在那裡驚呼了一分鐘。那裡有腳踏車紅綠燈、自行車道，所有基本的還有其他的都有。而且我也覺得看著腳踏車上的人們打扮好去上班很有趣。他們真的是騎腳踏車也要很有風格。

Becca
貝卡

I was in Berlin and my Airbnb host left me a bike to explore the city. I thought that was very nice of him, so I took the bike out and biked around the city. There were a lot of people biking around the city, and it was a really good way to get to know the city. Berlin stuck me as a top student in class, but he also dresses very nicely and very chic. What was my point...I just lost my train of thought.

我在柏林的時候，我 Airbnb 的主人留了一輛腳踏車給我去探索那個城市。我那時候覺得他人很好，於是我就帶了腳踏車出去蹓躂。那裡也有很多人在騎腳踏車，而且我覺得那真的是一個認識那個城市的好方式。柏林讓我覺得他好像是一個班上頂尖的學生，但是又很會打扮很時髦。我想說的是什麼…我的思路亂掉了啦。

02
Question

Do you enjoy touring by bike? Why? Why not?

你喜歡用腳踏車觀光嗎？為什麼或是為什麼不喜歡？

Michelle
蜜雪兒

I like it, but it's not my top choice. There are some advantages of touring by bike. It's really easy to park them, and the breeze is nice. However, on the other hand, if it's a hot day, then it'll ruin your trip. I'll just ride to the nearest coffee shop and call it a day.

我喜歡，可是那不是我最喜歡的選項。用腳踏車觀光有很多好處。很好停車，然後微風也很舒服。但是，另外一方面來說，如果今天很熱的話，那就會毀了你的旅程。我應該會騎到最近的咖啡店，然後就結束今天的行程。

Matt
麥特

I love touring by bike if I'm given the choice. You can go wherever you go without worrying too much about traffic jams. You don't hide yourself on the bike. On the contrary, you're exposed to the place. You have to say hi to people and you have to listen, and smell the place. I understand it could go both good and bad in that sense, but for me I'm willing to take the risks.

如果可以的話我非常喜歡用腳踏車觀光。你可以去任何地方然後也不用太擔心塞車，而且你在腳踏車上面沒辦法躲起來。相反的，你是暴露在那個地方的。你遇到認識的人的時候一定要打招呼，你也一定要聽或是聞這個地方。我知道那樣可能會很好或是很不好。但是我會想要冒那個險，用這種方式體驗這個城市。

Becca
貝卡

Yes, I do actually. It's cheap and you can see a lot when you are on a bike, too! Of course I can't go as far as when

騎
自
行
車

I'm in the car, but I think a bike will do. It's just a very organic way to tour around the place, and really slow down to see what is around you.

嗯，我真的很喜歡。因為它是很便宜的方式，而且在腳踏車上你也可以看到很多。我當然是不會像在開車的時候一樣去那麼遠，但是我想腳踏車就夠了啦。那是一種很有機的觀光方式，而且同時間也可以慢下來並且看看在你身邊的事物。

03 Question

Have you ever ridden racing bikes, mountain bikes, BMX bikes or other recreational bikes?
你有騎過公路車、登山車、BMX 整車或是其它休閒腳踏車嗎？

Michelle
蜜雪兒

How do you call regular bikes? I usually just ride those, and they work great for a ride down the street or touring around the city. I've never ridden a mountain bike or a racing bike before because I'm just not that type of girl. I don't ride with dirt. I ride with my high heels.

你怎麼叫那些一般的腳踏車啊？我通常就是騎那些，而且如果只是要騎到附近街上或是觀光城市，那是還蠻棒的方式啦。我從來沒騎過登山車或是公路車因為我就不是那種女生。我不喜歡跟土一起騎車，我喜歡跟我的高跟鞋一起騎。

Matt
麥特

Yeah, I've joined a few iron man races, and cycling is actually my strongest one. I also mountain biked a few times here and there when I'm traveling. It's really exciting and they are just great exercises. Biking just makes me feel so free and I guess I like the exercise, too!

有啊，我有參加過幾個三項鐵人的競賽。騎腳踏車是我的強項。我也有在旅行的時候騎過幾次登山車。真的很刺激，也是很好的經驗。騎腳踏車會讓我覺得好自由，而且我想我也很喜歡那個運動啦。

Becca
貝卡

I mean, I ride bikes, but nothing too crazy. I have a beach cruiser that is nice to cruise around, but it is horrible when you need to go up hills. There are no gears on that bike. I love my bike, but I just might sell it.

我是說，我騎腳踏車，但是沒有很瘋狂的那種。我有一個可以很好處晃晃的海灘腳踏車，但是如果要爬坡的話就超爛的。因為它是單速腳踏車。我很愛我的腳踏車可是我應該會賣掉它。

 Useful expressions

⚓ pick your brains 請教

❶ I have no ideas about how to write this assignment. Do you mind if I pick on your brains after school?

我完全不知道該怎麼寫這次的作業。你介不介意放學之後我跟你請教一下？

⚓ for your information 提供給你參考，跟你說一下

❷ For your information, he is not in the best mood today.

跟你說一下，他今天心情沒有很好。

⛵ **out of the way** 處理完畢，完成

❸ I'm so glad to get the work out of the way. Now it's time for some fun!

我好高興終於做完工作了。現在我們來玩吧！

⛵ **bike friendly** 很適合騎腳踏車的

❹ This city is not very bike friendly. There is no way for anyone to ride bikes here.

這個城市真的很不適合騎腳踏車。沒有人可以在這裡騎腳踏車的！

⛵ **jaw dropping** 令人掉下巴的，令人震驚的

❺ It was a jaw dropping experience to see how much the city transformed.

看到這個城市轉變得那麼劇烈真是令人掉下巴。

⛵ **train of thought** 思路

❻ She is always all over the place and it's really hard to follow her train of thought.

她總是很無厘頭，而且真的很難跟著她的思路走。

⛵ **call it a day** 結束今天的行程

❼ It started to rain and we just decided to call it a day.

那時候開始下雨，所以我們就決定要結束那天的行程了。

 背景起源

Just like everything else in life, there are a growing number of options for accommodation as well. Basic or luxurious, shared or private rooms, oceanfront or with mountain views...etc. It all comes down to what you are looking for in accommodation. Everyone seems to understand that hotels can be rather limited to people with more budget, and thus people come up with a lot of creative accommodation options nowadays, such as CouchSurfing, Airbnb, VRBO. After all, accommodation can be the major part of your traveling budget. Some with the feature of local knowledge, travelers can enjoy their stay with a much more local experience. Nevertheless, calculate the risks when you go for options including staying at someone's house. Enjoy your stay!

就像生活中很多其他的事一樣，住宿也有越來越多的選項。基本還是豪華，分住還是私人套房，面海還是山景等等。到頭來都還是取決於你的需求。大家好像都漸漸瞭解飯店比較侷限於預算比較多的人，於是現在就開始想出一些比較有創意的住宿方式，例如當沙發客、Airbnb 民宿，還是 VRBO 渡假租屋。因為畢竟住宿佔了你旅遊預算的一大部分。有些方式主打當地人的玩法，遊客可以以比較當地人的方式住宿停留。不過如果你決定要選擇住在別人家，一定要計算好風險。住得愉快喔！

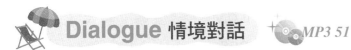 **Dialogue 情境對話** MP3 51

Paul is checking in a hostel in Barcelona.
保羅正在巴塞隆納的一間青年旅社 check in。

Paul: Hola, I have a reservation under Paul Brown.

保羅：嗨（西文），我有用保羅柏朗這個名字訂一間房間。

Anna the clerk: Hola Paul, my name is Anna! Can I see your passport?

安娜（櫃檯）：嗨（西文）保羅，我叫安娜！我可以看你的護照嗎？

Paul: Sure, here you are. Sorry to come in so late.

保羅：當然可以，在這裡。不好意思這麼晚才來。

住宿

Anna: No problem. We have a lot of visitors coming in at this time, too. Is this your first time in Barcelona?

安娜：沒關係。我們有很多遊客也是這時候才來。這是你第一次來巴塞隆納嗎？

Paul: Yeah, it is my first time. I'm very excited!

保羅：對啊，這是我第一次來。我很興奮耶！

Anna: Oh great! Welcome! I'll give you a map and some suggestions. Let me show you around at the lounge area and the computer area. We have Wifi, too, if you need it for your phone or other devices.

安娜：喔太好了！歡迎！我會給你一張地圖跟一些建議。讓我帶你看一下我們的休憩區和電腦區。如果你的電話還是其他設備需要的話，我們也有 wifi 喔！

Paul: Great, thank you so much! Wow, there are still many people here at this hour.

保羅：太好了！謝謝你！哇，這麼晚了還有這麼多人在這裡。

Anna: Yes, this group had just come in before you. They are going to a local tapas bar if you want to join them!

安娜：對啊，這群人也是剛在你來之前到的。如果你想加入他們的話，他們要去一間當地的西班牙小酒吧喔！

Paul: Yes, that will be wonderful to meet some friends I think. Thanks for the tips and I will try and ask if I can join them to the tapas bar.

保羅：喔好啊，交一些新朋友也是不錯！謝謝你的提示還有我會去問他們我可以不可以加入！

Anna: We have breakfast here at 8 a.m. If you would like to eat, and we have a few historical walking tours at 10 am if you care to join tomorrow morning.

安娜：如果你想吃東西的話，我們早上八點有早餐，然後十點會有一個歷史的徒步行程如果你想加入的話。

Paul: Thanks Anna for all your help!

保羅：謝謝你的幫忙安娜！

 三問三答　*MP3 52*

01 Question

What type of accommodation do you usually stay in when you travel? Why?
你旅行的時候通常都比較喜歡哪一種住宿方式？為什麼？

I usually just go with the hotels. It's easy and safe, and really, do you really want to clean up your mess before you leave when you are on vacation? Pay a little bit extra to get the peace of mind. I think it's worth it.

我通常都會選擇住飯店。又簡單又安全，而且說真的，你真的想要在度假時離開前還要打掃嗎？付多一點換來一點心安，我是覺得很值得啦。

Couchsurfing for sure. I know how some people would have concerns about the safety of Couchsurfing, but the website has so many safety measures in play. It's really not bad at all. I love Couchsurfing because that's where the magic of traveling happens. You get to mingle with your local host and possibly their friends. It, in a way, is forcing you to make friends, and I like that idea.

　　我一定是選沙發衝浪。我知道有些人會對沙發衝浪有安全的考量，但是其實它網站上有做了許多安全的措施。其實沒那麼糟。我很愛沙發衝浪，因為那就是旅行神奇的地方。你可以跟當地的主人或是主人的朋友交流。而且其實沙發衝浪有一點強迫你去交朋友，我真的很喜歡那樣。

Becca
貝卡

　　I like to use Airbnb. It's usually a good deal if you play it right. And different from Couchsurfing, you don't always see your host. Most of the time they just give you a separate room or even the whole place to yourself. I like the price and I also want my privacy.

　　我喜歡用 Airbnb. 其實你用對戰術的話，它通常都是很便宜的。而且跟沙發衝浪不同的是，你不一定會見到你的住宿主人。大部分時候他們都會給你另外一間房間，或甚至是留整個地方給你。我喜歡它的價錢，也想要我自己的隱私。

住宿

Do you have any interesting stories at the accommodation when you were traveling?

你有沒有一些旅行的時候關於住宿有趣的故事？

Michelle
蜜雪兒

I was staying at the Four Seasons Hotel in Miami and found out that a local celebrity and his family were staying next to my room. I didn't really know him since I didn't really watch TV that much, but from what the housekeepers told me, he was really popular, but he was a very difficult customer.

我在邁阿密的時候住在四季酒店，然後發現隔壁住的是當地的名人和他的家人。我不認識他因為我沒什麼在看電視，但飯店的管家跟我說，他在當地很受歡迎，但他真是一個大奧客。

Matt
麥特

Once I was on a hiking trip in Europe. I didn't have Internet to book my hostel, so I could only go to the hostel after I finished the hike that day. It was after sunset, and the only hostel in the town was all booked out. They only had one private room available, but it would cost me 60 dollars. I didn't have that much budget, so sadly I had to leave. However, miraculously, the owner of the hostel asked me if I could help him fold the sheets, and if I helped him, I could get the room for free. So I did it happily, and miraculously earned my private room and a great night sleep for free.

有一次我去歐洲健行旅行。我身上沒有網路可以訂青年旅社,所以我只好健行完再去青年旅社訂房間。那時候已經是日落,而且那間鎮上唯一的一間青年旅社房間也完全被訂完了。他們只剩下一間單人房,但是一間要價六十元美金。我沒有那麼多預算,所以只好難過的要離開。但神奇的是,青年旅社的主人突然問我可不可以幫他折床單,他說如果我可以幫他的話,我就可以免費住在那個房間。所以我就很高興地幫他折床單,而且奇蹟似地賺到我的單人房,還有一覺好眠。

So there are times when you cannot hide from your host from Airbnb. This is one of the examples. I went to the meeting place to get my room key from my host in India. However, she insisted that I should join her for their family reunion that evening. <u>The next thing I knew</u>, I was sitting in the middle of a big Indian family and taking family photos.

有時候你沒辦法躲過你的 Airbnb 住宿主人。這就是其中的一個例子。我在印度去了約好見面的地方跟住宿主人拿鑰匙。但是，她堅持要我加入她們家晚上的家族聚會。我反應過來的時候，我就坐在一個印度大家族的中間，跟她們拍家族合照。

03 Question
What do you care the most about your accommodation?
你對住宿最重視的是什麼？

Service! Duh! It is fair to demand great service when you pay quite a bit of money. I'm not trying to be difficult, but the whole point of traveling is that you want to enjoy your vacation. Otherwise, I can just stay home. Do you see where I'm coming from?

當然是服務囉！當你花那麼多錢的時候，我覺得要求好的服務是很公平的。我不是想當奧客，但是旅行的目的不就是要享受嗎？不然我就待在家就好啦。你懂我的邏輯嗎？

I always go with the host that can offer the most local experiences. Isn't it the whole point of traveling? To see other culture and what people do in difference places? Since I always Couchsurf, local experiences would be the things I am constantly looking for.

我都是選有提供當地體驗的住宿主人。那就是旅行的重點不是嗎？去看其他的文化還有人們在不一樣的地方做的事情。因為我是沙發客，所以有沒有當地體驗就是我找住宿的重點。

Becca
貝卡

As much as I like to budget myself, I really care about how clean a place is. It doesn't have to be spotless, but it has to be at least clean and livable. I don't want to get <u>bitten by the</u> "real" <u>travel bug</u> home.

就算我很小心花錢，我真的很重視一個地方乾不乾淨。不用到一塵不染，可是至少要整潔和可以住人。我不想要被「真的」旅遊蟲子咬到。

Useful **expressions**

⛵ **it all comes down to** 這都是取決於⋯

❶ It all comes down to money in the end.

最後這些都是取決於錢。

⚓ **that's where the magic happens** 那就是…神奇的地方

❷ Step out of your comfort zone because that's where the magic happens.

你應該要踏出你的舒適圈，因為好事都是在舒適圈外發生的。

⚓ **the next thing I know** 我反應過來之後就…

❸ I fell asleep on the way home. I remembered coming in the car after dinner. The next thing I knew, we were in front of our house already.

我在回家的路上睡著了。我記得吃完晚餐回到車上。等我反應過來，我們已經在家門口了。

⚓ **bitten by the travel bug** 迷上了旅遊

❹ I fee like I have been bitten by the travel bug. I can't stop thinking about the next traveling destination.

我覺得我好像已經迷上旅遊了。我沒辦法停止想著下一個旅行的地方。

住宿

Transportation
運輸

 背景起源

There are so many ways to travel around the world, and most of the time, your budget will determine which type of transportation you will use in the end. Anything from flying, to a cruise to using local transportation. Whichever option you choose, you need to make sure that it is suitable for you, and you only. It is part of your trip after all. Overall, planning your journey is essential and being realistic about what you can do for your budget is important, too. You don't want to spend thousands of dollars on transportation and then starve and not be able to do anything in the country!

　　有很多不一樣的辦法可以讓你到世界各地旅遊，但是大多數時間，你的預算會決定了你最後的交通方式是什麼。從飛機、遊輪，到使用當地交通工具，不管你最後選了那一個選項，你一定要確保那是適合你，也是專屬於你的選擇。那畢竟是你旅行的一部分。大致上來說，計劃你的行程是必要的，而且你也必須對你的預算可以做的事情現實一點。你不會想要花大錢在交通工具上，但是到了當地卻餓肚子或是什麼事也不能做。

 **Dialogue 情境對話** MP3 53

Robert is taking a taxi from the airport to his hotel in India. His driver is Tilak.

羅柏正在印度的機場搭了一輛計程車要到他的飯店。他的司機的名字是提拉克。

Tilak: Good morning sir, my name is Tilak. Where do you want to go?

提拉克：早安，先生。我的名字是提拉克。你想要去哪裡呢？

Robert: Please take me to the Hilton New Delhi Hotel.

羅柏：請帶我到希爾頓新德里飯店。

Tilak: No problem, sir.

提拉克：沒問題，先生。

Robert: Wow, be careful Tilak. The traffic is pretty bad here, right?

羅柏：哇，小心阿提拉克！這裡的交通蠻差的啊？

Tilak: Yes, sir. There is always a lot going on here.

提拉克：對啊，先生。路上總是蠻多狀況的。

Robert: Are those cows in the middle of the road?

羅柏：在路中間的那些是牛嗎？

Tilak: Yes, sir. They are very holy animals, so we cannot shush them away.

提拉克：是的先生。他們是非常神聖的動物，所以我們不可以噓他們走。

Robert: Watch out!!! There is someone running across the street. How can you drive here? There is so much going on on the road. Cars, Tuk Tuks, bikes, pedestrians, cows...

羅柏：小心！！！！有人剛跑過馬路。你怎麼有辦法在這裡開車？路上真的太多狀況了！車子、嘟嘟車、腳踏車、行人、牛…

Tilak: You'll get used to it after a while.

提拉克：你過一陣子就會習慣了。

Robert: I can understand why everyone is honking constantly now.

羅柏：我現在可以聊解為什麼大家都一直按喇叭了！

Tilak: Yeah, it's a way to communicate, but mostly to tell people to get away!

提拉克：對啊，那其實是溝通的一種辦法，但是大部分的時間我們是在說讓開！

Robert: I see. I also realize something else that's interesting.

羅柏：嗯嗯我懂。我也發現還有另一件事情是蠻有趣的。

Tilak: What is that sir?

提拉克：是什麼事呢先生？

Rober: Your driver's seat is on the left, and you drive on the left as well. In my country, our driver seat is on the left, but we drive on the right side of the road.

羅柏：你們的駕駛座是在左邊，而且你們也是開在路的左邊。在我的國家，我們的駕駛座是在左邊，但是我們開車是開在路的右邊。

Tilak: Oh...no sir. We "should" drive on the right side of the road technically...

提拉克：喔…不是的先生。我們其實「應該要」開在路的右邊啦…

 三問三答 　　MP3 54

運輸

01 Question

What forms of transportation do you usually use when you are traveling? Why?

你在旅行的時候通常會用什麼交通工具？為什麼？

Michelle
蜜雪兒

I usually go with the driver guide service. I really don't <u>feel like</u> handling the stress of looking for directions or getting lost when I'm traveling. I just want to use the time in the most efficient way. If someone can drive for me and take me to the spots I'm interested in with local knowledge, it's like I have a friend in that country. In a way, I hire a local friend for my vacation.

我通常會選擇司機兼導遊的服務。我真的很不想要在旅行的時候還要煩惱找路，或是迷路。我只是想要有效率地利用時間。如果有人可以幫我開車，還可以帶我到我有興趣的地方去玩，那就好像是我在那個國家有一個當地的朋友一樣。其實就好像是我為了我的假期僱用了一個當地的朋友啦。

Matt
麥特

I usually <u>hitchhike</u> when I'm traveling. You will be amazed at how many kind people there are in the world.

Sometimes it only takes me 5 minutes to get a ride, but sometimes it takes a couple of hours. It was hard for me to hitchhike at the beginning because I couldn't handle the rejection, but it's just silly thinking back.

我在旅行的時候通常喜歡搭便車。你會很驚訝世界上有多少好人。有的時候只會花五分鐘，可是有的時候要等好幾個小時。一開始的時候其實搭便車對我來說很難，因為我不喜歡被拒絕的感覺，但是現在回想過去我真的是很傻。

Becca
貝卡

It really depends on where I go. There are a lot of places that have metro systems. It's cheap and it's quick. Local people use it, too. If I need to go somewhere remote, I'll go with Uber. It's a new thing though, it's pretty much an app you can request rides from where you are. It's usually cheaper than a taxi, so there you go!

真的要看我是去哪裡。其實很多地方都有地鐵。它又便宜又快。當地人也會使用它。如果我要去很遙遠的地方的話，我就會用 Uber。不過那個還蠻新的。其實它就是一個 APP 你可以在你所在的地方叫車。

運輸

而且通常他還比計程車便宜，當然是選他囉！

02
Question

What are some local transportation you took and thought they were cool?
你有沒有坐過什麼當地的交通工具，然後覺得他們很酷的？

Michelle
蜜雪兒

I was in Venice and of course I had to try the Gondola ride, but I went with the slightly fancier one. My gondola offered a private tour and it came with the singers and the musicians. It was really romantic, but I didn't really have a date, so it was actually a little bit awkward. Well, it was really cool though.

我在威尼斯的時候當然要試試看貢多拉，但是我是選了比一般高級一點點的。我的貢多拉有私人導覽，而且船上還有歌手和樂手。真的很浪漫但是我那個時候沒有伴啦，所以其實有點尷尬。不過還是蠻酷的就是了。

Matt
麥特

I was taking the Tuk Tuk in Vietnam and it wasn't really the safest ride I took. I felt like the vehicle was about to break at any time. Strange enough, I enjoyed my ride as my driver was weaving through the traffic in the middle of Ho Chi Minh City. It was a pretty unique experience.

我在越南的時候有坐嘟嘟車，它真的不是我坐過算很安全的。我覺得那車好像隨時都會垮掉一樣。很奇怪的是，我的司機在胡志明市中穿梭在車陣之間時，我其實是還蠻喜歡的。那是一個蠻獨特的體驗。

Becca
貝卡

I was in Florida riding the Segway while I was touring around. I felt like a really lazy person from the future, but it was really awesome. It was easy to control and it gets me to where I need to go without too much effort...Oh my god, I sound like a really lazy person from the future...

運輸

我在佛羅里達州的時候有用賽格威（電動代步車）到處遊覽。我那時候覺得我真的很像是從未來來的很懶惰的人，但是那真的很棒耶！它很簡單控制而且也很輕鬆就帶我到我需要去的地方…我的天啊，我聽起來好像是從未來來的很懶惰的人…

---

03 **Question**
Do you have any bad experience about transportation when you are traveling?
你旅行的時候有沒有遇過什麼關於交通工具不好的經驗？

Michelle
蜜雪兒

It wasn't bad, but it <u>caught me by surprise</u>. When I was in Bangkok, my friends and I wanted to go to this local bar far away, so naturally we wanted to take the taxi. It should be a great thing for the taxi driver, right? If we want to go somewhere far from where we got picked up. But no, no taxi drivers would take us because it was too far. We ended up going to a different bar.

是沒有很糟，可是有出乎我的意料之外。我在曼谷的時候，我的朋友和我想要去一個蠻遠的當地酒吧，所以很自然的我們想要搭計程車。

如果我們要去離我們上車很遠的地方，對計程車司機應該是很好不是嗎？但是不是，因為太遠了的關係，沒有計程車司機要帶我們去。我們最後只好換去一個不一樣的酒吧。

Matt
麥特

I was going to Alabama for a music festival, but I landed in Atlanta. I decided to go with Greyhound Bus, which turned out to be a total disaster. The bus never came and I had to catch a different bus to the Greyhound central station. Not only that, the bathroom on the bus was beyond horrible. I don't think I would take the bus again.

我要去阿拉巴馬州參加音樂節，可是我在亞特蘭大下飛機。我那時候決定要做灰狗巴士，結果後來變成一個大災難。那車沒來，所以我要做另外一輛公車到灰狗巴士的總站。不止那樣而已，車上的廁所恐怖的不得了。我想我應該不會再坐他們的公車。

運輸

Becca
貝卡

When my friends and I were looking for a taxi to go to our hostel in Vietnam, we tried to ask the taxi drivers if they were running by the meter (recommended by our friends), or we wouldn't take the taxi. No taxi driver would take us until this one guy took us. However, we soon discovered that the meter was broken. We had to ask him to <u>pull over</u> and he got really mad. Luckily there were people around where he stopped the car. That was pretty scary.

我跟我朋友要搭計程車到我們的青年旅社的時候，我們問了那裡的司機他們是不是照里程表算錢（我們的朋友建議的），不然的話，我們就不坐他們的車。沒有人要載我們，後來有一個司機說好。但是我們上車之後很快就發現他的里程表是壞掉的。我們叫他停在路邊，他超級生氣的。幸好他停車的地方有很多人。不過那真的蠻恐怖的。

Useful expressions

⛵ **You'll get used to it.** 你後來就會習慣的啦。

❶ It's a really hard job, but you'll get used to it.

這是一個很有挑戰性的工作，不過你後來就會習慣了啦。

⛵ get away 讓開

❷ Get away people! I can't drive that well!

大家快點讓開！我開車技術沒有很好！

⛵ feel like 想要

❸ I don't feel like going to bed now. We should go see a movie.

我不想要去睡覺了。我們應該要去看個電影。

⛵ hitchhike 搭便車

❹ You need to be careful when you hitchhike. You are a pretty girl.

你搭便車的時候要很小心喔。你那麼漂亮。

⛵ a couple of 幾個、一些

❺ I need a couple of days to finish this painting.

我需要幾天才可以完成這幅畫。

⛵ be caught by surprise 出乎意料

❻ When he proposed, I was really caught by surprise. I had no idea what he was going to do it.

他求婚的時候真的完全出乎我的意料之外。我完全不知道他要求婚。

運輸

Emergency
緊急事件

Unit

 背景起源

When people are sharing their travel stories, not only do the fun or the bubbly parts of your journey make great stories. Oftentimes, the emergencies you run into in your trips are the most memorable ones. They may not be the best outing experiences, but they will for sure be the most memorable adventures you keep talking about for the rest of your life. Why is that? We like to think it's perhaps because they do not happen that often or we should say they usually do not happen the way you expected it. And then all exciting and the adrenaline rushed moments come to an end, leaving us with a great lesson and awesome story to tell. Needless to say, no one favors emergency. However, such is life, we try our best to avoid it, and yet, when it comes, we deal with it with grace.

當大家在分享旅行的故事時，不只是那些好玩的美好的像泡泡般的部分是最好的故事。很多時候，那些你在旅行時遇到的緊急事件才是最令你難忘的故事。它們可能不是最棒的外出經驗，但是一定是讓你很難忘並且下半輩子一直跟別人說的冒險故事。為什麼呢？我們偏好認為是因為或許緊急事件不常發生，或者我們應該說沒有照你預期的發生。而當那些刺激、腎上腺素飆漲的時刻過了之後，它只留給我們一個很好的教訓，還有一個超棒的故事。不必說，沒有人喜歡緊急事件，可是人生就是這樣，我們盡可能地避免它，但是當緊急事件發生的時候，我們也要處之泰然。

Dialogue 情境對話　MP3 55

Amanda and Michael are checking in a hotel in India when she found out that she lost her passport.
艾曼達和麥可正要在印度的一家飯店 check in，可是艾曼達發現她的護照不見了。

Amanda: Just a second. Sorry I have so much stuff in my bag, and I will never find anything in this bag.

艾曼達：等一下喔。對不起我有好多東西在我的包包裡。在這包包裡我永遠都找不到任何東西。

Michael: Haha...That's okay, as long as you find the passport. It is just a little important. We have to leave for

麥可：哈哈…沒關係，只要你找得到你的護照就好了。這只有一點點

緊急事件

Bali tomorrow.

的重要。我們明天就要
飛峇厘島了。

Amanda: Yeah, I know, Michael. You were not helping...Hang on. I think I really lost my passport this time.

艾曼達：對啊，我知道。麥可，你沒有幫到忙喔…等等。我覺得我這次好像真的弄丟我的護照了。

Michael: Stop joking around. Come on Amanda. Let's check in and go explore the city a little bit.

麥可：不要再開玩笑了啦！艾曼達快點啦，我們趕快 Check in 然後去看看這個城市。

Amanda: For once I'm not joking. I've looked everywhere. Help me out here Michael. I need your help.

艾曼達：這次我沒在開玩笑。我到處都找過了。幫我找啦麥可。我需要你的幫忙！

Michael: Cut it out Amanda! This is really not funny...Are you serious? What? Give me your bag.

麥可：不要鬧了艾曼達！真的很冷耶…你是認真的嗎？什麼？給我你的包包。

(After both of them going through all Amanda's bags)

（在他們兩個都找遍了艾曼達的包包後）

Amanda: What should I do? Our flight is tomorrow. I'm so sorry Michael. If anything, go without me, and I'll find my way there.

艾曼達：我該怎麼辦？我們是搭明天的飛機耶。對不起啦麥可。不過萬一沒辦法的話，你就先走，我會再想辦法過去。

Michael: Don't be silly. I'm sure there's an American Embassy here. Let's call them and see what the options are. I'm sure this happens all the time.

麥可：別傻了。這裡一定有美國大使館。我們打電話給他們問問看我們該怎麼做。這一定常常發生。

Amanda: That people lost their passports? I'm such a mess. Michael, I'm so sorry.

艾曼達：你說大家弄丟護照常常發生嗎？我真是一團亂耶麥可，對不起啦。

Michael: Don't worry about it. Now let's move on and fix it together. It's not the end of the world, come on.

麥可：別擔心了啦。現在我們繼續往前一起解決，這又不是世界末日，拜託。

Amanda: What did I do to deserve you?

艾曼達：我到底燒了什麼好香可以有你在我身邊？

緊急事件

341

Michael: You cook well.　　　　　　麥可：你煮飯很好吃。

三問三答　MP3 56

01
Question

Have you ever encountered any emergency during your trip? What happened?
你有曾經在旅行的時候遇到什麼緊急事件嗎？發生了什麼事？

Michelle
蜜雪兒

Once when I was traveling to the Caribbean, it took me two days to get there and seven days for my bags to arrive! You can only imagine my dismay. I was utterly destroyed inside. I had bought and matched up all my outfits for my Caribbean trip before I left. Also, all my toiletry and skincare products were all in the luggage. I had to go shopping all over again for the first two days. I didn't mind doing the shopping, but you know how it is with skincare products. There are only certain brands that are perfect for you. It was just depressing thinking about it again.

有一次我到加勒比海旅行，花了我兩天的時間才飛到目的地，但是我的行李七天才到！你可以想像我有多沮喪。我內心完全崩潰。在我出發到加勒比海之前，我已經買好了衣服，也都搭配好每天要穿的了。而且，我的盥洗用品和保養品也都在行李裡。我前兩天都要到處去逛街。逛街我是不介意，可是你知道保養品。他們就是只有某些牌子是完全適合你的。我現在想到就又開始沮喪了。

Matt
麥特

I was <u>food poisoned</u> when I was in Cusco. It was bad because I was traveling by myself, and I couldn't do anything besides puking and having diarrhea for the first few days. It was scary because I was too weak to go seek for help of any sort. I was just sleeping, woke up to puke and then passed out again. Luckily all the bacteria must have eventually got out of my system, but it was just a bad experience.

我在庫斯科的時候食物中毒。那時候很慘因為我只有一個人在旅行，而且我前幾天除了吐和拉肚子之外完全無法做其他事。那時候很可怕因為我虛弱到完全無法去求救。我就只有睡覺，醒來去吐，然後又昏睡過去。好險最後細菌總算完全脫離我的身體，但那還是一個很糟的經驗。

Becca
貝卡

My friends and I rented a car and we parked it with all the other cars by the road and we went hiking. After we were done hiking, our car was broken into. The windows were broken and our bags were stolen. I hid my wallet in the car and the thieves found it, so I had to cancel all my credit cards, but luckily I didn't have much cash in the wallet. We reported the incident and took the car back to the rental company to switch for a new one since we had purchased the insurance at the beginning.

我朋友跟我租了一台車,我們停在路邊其他車旁,然後我們就去爬山了。我們回來的時候,發現有人打破我們的車子。窗戶都破了,而我們的包包都被偷了。我把我的皮夾藏在車子裡,但是小偷找到了,所以我要掛失一堆信用卡,但是好險我皮夾裡沒有很多現金。我們報了警之後因為一開始有買保險,所以就把車帶回租車的地方換了一輛新的。

02
Question

What would be the worst thing that could happen for you during the trip? Why?
你最怕旅行的時候會發生什麼事？為什麼？

Michelle
蜜雪兒

Needless to say, losing my bags again would seriously be the worst thing ever. Surprisingly, this kind of thing happens so much. I did some research and wrote a complaint letter to the airlines, but apparently almost everyone has a friend that lost their luggage before. How 's that?

不用說，當然就是再弄丟我的行李一次會是最糟的。很令人傻眼的是，這很常發生耶。我有查了一下然後就寫了一封抱怨信給航空公司，但是好像幾乎大家都有一個朋友有弄丟過行李。怎麼樣，很令人驚訝吧？

緊急事件

There are a lot of bad things that can happen when you are on the road. I think for me, getting seriously injured would definitely be the worst. There's nothing more important than health. Without it, you can't travel anywhere.

你在旅行的時候有很多不好的事有可能會發生。我覺得對我來說最糟的就是受了重傷。沒有什麼事比健康更重要了。沒有健康，你不能去任何地方旅行。

Becca
貝卡

For girls, I think the worst thing that could happen is guys with very bad intentions. There's really not much you can do when you are in those kinds of situations. Not to be a sexist, most guys are physically stronger than us. I personally think I'm somewhat attractive, too, so...

我覺得對女生來說，最糟的就是遇到不懷好意的男生。在那些情況下你真的也沒有什麼辦法了。我也不是要作性別歧視，不過大部分的男生都比女生還要強壯很多。我個人是覺得我還有點姿色，所以…

Do you do anything as a precaution to prevent emergencies for your trips?
你有做什麼事來預防旅行的時候緊急事件發生嗎？

Question **03**

Michelle
蜜雪兒

I started to pack one third of my clothes, mini toiletry and skincare products in my carryon bags and the rest in the luggage ever since that horrible incident happened in the Caribbean. Oh, and it's also a good idea to put your money in different places or bags. If you lose one, at least you still have some in other bags. Yeah, they didn't call me a travel expert for no reason.

我自從上次在加勒比海發生那件恐怖的事後，我就開始放三分之一的衣服，迷你的盥洗用品還有保養品在隨身行李裡，然後剩下的再放在托寄行李裡。喔，還有就是要把你的錢放在不一樣的地方，這樣一來，如果你丟掉一筆的話，至少你在其他地方還有錢。沒錯，他們不是平白

無故叫我旅遊專家的。

I make extra copies of my passport and visas and put them in different places just in case I lose them. Losing your passport can be a pain in the butt when you are traveling, and unfortunately it happens quite often.

我有多影印了幾份護照和簽證，然後再把它們放在不一樣的包包裡以防我弄丟了護照。在旅行的時候弄丟護照真的超煩的，而且很不幸的是那還很常發生。

I always carry hand sanitizers and avoid eating foods by the street. I took necessary and unnecessary vaccines, stomach medicines, pepper spray, and oh a fake wedding ring!!

我都會隨身攜帶乾洗手液還有不吃路邊的食物。我也會打必要跟不必要的疫苗，帶胃藥、防狼噴霧器，噢對了！還有一個假的結婚戒指！

 Useful expressions

⚓ **such is life 這就是人生**

❶ I don't like to work so hard, either, but such is life. What can you do?

我也不喜歡工作的那麼辛苦啊，但是這就是人生。你還能怎麼辦呢？

⚓ **cut it out 不要鬧了**

❷ Cut it out! Ray! I'm trying to focus here.

不要鬧了！雷！我試著要專心一點。

⚓ **I'm a mess. 我真是一團亂**

❸ You don't want to hang out with me now. I'm a mess.

你現在不會想要跟我一起玩。我現在是一團亂。

⚓ **What did I do to deserve you? 我到底是做了什麼好事可以才擁有你？**

❹ You are always so nice to me. What did I do to deserve you?

你總是對我那麼好。我到底是做了什麼好事才可以擁有你？

Learn Smart! 053

愛玩客的旅遊英語 (MP3)

作　　者	李佩玲 Bella
封面構成	高鍾琪
內頁構成	菩薩蠻數位文化有限公司

發 行 人	周瑞德
執行總監	齊心瑀
企劃編輯	陳韋佑
執行編輯	魏于婷
校　　對	陳欣慧、饒美君
印　　製	大亞彩色印刷製版股份有限公司
初　　版	2015 年 12 月
定　　價	新台幣 380 元
出　　版	倍斯特出版事業有限公司
電　　話	(02) 2351-2007
傳　　真	(02) 2351-0887
地　　址	100 台北市中正區福州街 1 號 10 樓之 2
E - m a i l	best.books.service@gmail.com
網　　址	www.bestbookstw.com

港澳地區總經銷	泛華發行代理有限公司
地　　　　址	香港新界將軍澳工業邨駿昌街 7 號 2 樓
電　　　　話	(852) 2798-2323
傳　　　　真	(852) 2796-5471

國家圖書館出版品預行編目(CIP)資料

愛玩客的旅遊英語 / 李佩玲著. -- 初版. --
臺北市 : 倍斯特, 2015.12 面 ; 公分. --
(Learn smart;53)ISBN 978-986-91915-6-2
(平裝附光碟片)
1.英語 2.旅遊 3.會話
805.188　　　　　　　　104025147